HONESTLY

by

LYNNE PATRICIA DOUCETTE

HONESTLY

Copyright 2015 by Lynne Patricia Doucette

Published by
HeartBeat Productions Inc.
Box 633
Abbotsford, BC
Canada V2T 6Z8
email: heartbeatproductions@gmail.com
604.852.3761

Library and Archives Canada Cataloguing in Publication

Doucette, Lynne Patricia, 1957-, author
Honestly / by Lynne Patricia Doucette

Short stories.
Issued in print and electronic formats.
ISBN 978-1-523900-91-6 (pbk.).—ISBN 978-1-895112-21-4 (pdf)

I. Title.

PS8607.O9145H65 2015   C813'.6   C2015-902795-0
C2015-902796-9

Printed in USA

DEDICATION

For Jesus Christ, my Lord, my Saviour, my Healer, my Beloved.
Thank You for my life and second chances.
Thank you for the cross; Your pledge of love and grace.
I love You with all that I am.

FORWARD

Most of us go through one major crisis in life.
For some, it is the end of all hope. For others it is what
forges us, tests our mettle, solidifies our character and our
determination.
This book is about the latter group: those who dig in deeper,
suck the marrow from their circumstances and receive beauty
for ashes.

FOUR STORIES

TIGER DOORS

*For Shirley, whose honesty and straightforward manner
are a constant source of encouragement and peace.
I trust you implicitly, my friend, my sister in Christ. You are a
true reflection of His love.*

CONTENTS

PROLOGUE

Rolf steered the Jeep™ toward the mountains. They would be at the lake before nightfall. He and his son would have three days of fishing before heading back late Monday, the last day of the Canadian Thanksgiving long weekend. It had been a hectic day, a hectic Summer and Fall for that matter, but he was finally able to get away – to have some time to himself – to do what he wanted, with Damien, just the two of them...

He congratulated himself for beating the holiday traffic out of town. He had loaded the Jeep™ with camping and fishing gear that morning, left work early and had picked Damien up from school. The weather was warm for southern British Columbia in October... a delayed Indian Summer. The trees were splashed with reds and golds that flashed in the afternoon sun as they sped by them on the highway. The blue sky had thin, lazy clouds, high above the mountain range. It was perfect.

Forty-five minutes later, they were making their ascent around hairpin curves and over bumpy logging roads, to his favourite spot on Mirror Lake. Eleven year old Damien had drifted off to sleep soon after they had left the highway. His dark hair fell over his lashes as his head bobbed gently. A pang of regret washed over Rolf as he recalled the things he had said to his wife Katy that morning.

He immediately set out to defend his comments in his own mind. She had no idea the strain he was under at work. Besides, if she would only do things his way, there wouldn't be any arguments. Why did she have to be so stubborn? He clenched the steering wheel and turned red recalling how he had told her if she filed for divorce, he would never let her have Damien. Never.

Just then a yellow-jacket flew in the window and Rolf tried to squash it against the inside of the windshield without waking Damien. The crazy insect flew back and forth above the dashboard, just out of his reach. When it landed on Damien's lip,

Rolf took his eyes off the road momentarily, to shoo it away and looked back just in time to miss a logging truck whose lane he had swerved into.

Now in a cold sweat, he swore under his breath and suddenly remembered that his bee kit was in the glove box of his Mustang™ back at home. He had borrowed his friend, Jeff's Jeep™ and had forgotten to transfer it over.

Cursing again at his own stupidity, Rolf accelerated without thinking, matching his mood. He thought he saw the bee on his lower pant leg and bent down hitting his leg hard enough to kill a tarantula. He then looked up to see nothing but air in front of him and he screamed, "D-a-m-i-e-n!"

CHAPTER ONE

JUXTAPOSITION

O thou afflicted, tossed with tempest, *and* not comforted, behold, I will lay thy stones with fair colours, and lay thy foundations with sapphires. Isaiah 54:11

Ten months later...

It was mid-morning when Katy stumbled out of bed and into the semi-dark, designer living room... though the opulent plum decor bore no pleasure for her now. She sank onto the sofa and stretched her head back and took a deep breath. She closed her eyes, and willed her indolent thoughts into line; but she still saw the elusive, tiny, fuzzy particles; like fairies dancing and spinning before her in a wild suicidal blitz. One by one they popped, yet millions remained beckoning her focus. She couldn't concentrate on any of them. Stretching her neck back even further, she inhaled again, but oxygen was not to be her tonic. Still the madness raged. Even if she opened her eyes, she knew they would be there. They were always there. She could sense them, *feel* them. And always accompanying them were random snippets of thoughts, long-lost phrases she had heard or perhaps said herself, she wasn't sure, wafting through the swirl. But she couldn't grab any of them. She couldn't focus on anything for very long.

Mercifully she was snatched from the frenzy by a roaring garbage truck taking the corner up the street, and Katy moaned, "I suppose I should take the trash out." She gathered only the most critical debris scattered about her demure house, into a 'Saving-You-More' bag, and made her way outside.

Barefoot and squinting, she exited the side door off her kitchen to a porch and then took the stairs carefully, picking her way along the quaint cottage's flagstone side-path, mostly unconcerned whether she actually *caught* the truck or not. Moving slowly, with her dull, blonde hair hanging partially over her empty eyes, she smoothed a frail hand over her sweat-suited torso and pale legs. She knew she looked ill, and she was, though not in body.

The truck was approaching her driveway, when a rider bounded off the back and deftly retrieved her bag. "I'll take that Ma'am," the tanned youth gushed. He was wearing a tangerine muscle shirt, cut-offs, and what seemed to Katy, an inappropriate smile. She surmised, *Obviously a college student. A summer relief-worker.* She watched him scale the back of the beast while throwing the bag inside its cavernous belly. And then he was gone.

It wasn't like he owed it to her to match her mood. Why did his cheerfulness annoy her? she puzzled, shaking her head slightly. Katy sighed and turned back toward the house, pivoting once to watch the truck's withdrawal, carrying with it the residue of her last week's existence… carrying it to no-man's-land.

"Meoww. Meowwww?"

Katy was summoned from her observation by a mammoth, orange, tom cat that had wend its way around her legs, and was proceeding up the walk toward her faded white clapboard cottage.

"Meowwww?" The creature turned, glancing up at her.

Mechanically, she reached down and stroked its fluffy fur with her gentle, un-manicured hands. "Why are you beseeching me?" she queried. "You look like you have a fine home elsewhere?" Her voice was quiet, and especially soft, reminding her of her earlier self.

"Rrreow", the cat responded in a lower, more beguiling tone.

"Poor baby," Katy clucked scratching his ears, "not a friend in the world, huh?"

She went into the house to fetch a saucer of milk and placed it on the side porch, where her supplicant paced impatiently.

She could hear the distant voice of her mother warning: "Don't feed stray cats dear, they'll *never* leave you alone after you do."

And..."Katy, I understand your compassion for the underdog, and 'under-*cat*', for that matter, but believe me honey, cats are opportunists. Even if they have a secure hearth and home, they are always on the lookout for alternate fare."

I probably would've had a zoo of my own, if it weren't for Dad's say-so in the matter. Then after I got married, Rolf's allergies dictated the 'no pet rule', Katy mused. "Well, here you go," she said matter-of-factly, and shut the door on the cat... and the world.

Early the next morning, Katy awoke to the imploring cry of the hungry cat. Its whine was increasing in volume and intensity by the second. She chose to ignore it only briefly before getting out of bed and padding to the side door off her kitchen.

"Mother warned me about you", she chided, opening the screen clad only in an extra long, baby blue tee-shirt. "Well, I can't say I didn't know any better," she shrugged, pouring the last of her milk into the saucer.

She lingered to watch the cat, enjoying his fetch. There was something luxurious about his manner that resonated with something deep inside of her. As the cat finished, it licked its chops and paws, and nonchalantly proceeded to enter the house, *her home*. Katy barred its progress with her leg, and shut it out with the door.

Then, feeling sorry for her actions, she re-opened the door partly and bent down to make amends. Scratching the cat's head, she cooed, "Now don't take offence, I'm sure your family is wondering where you are. It's for your own good. I'm only doing this because I care..." *Care? Gosh. I've done it now. Let someone into my realm... Someone? A cat.* "Shoo!" Katy raised her voice slightly, closing the door gently, but firmly this time.

Later on, Katy made mental list as she set about her morning routine. *Guess I'll have to get some groceries today. No milk, hmmm, no bread... what else?* Carefree birds were chirping merrily in the brilliance outside, but a dark shroud over the bathroom window limited their song, and the sun, to merely sneaking around its sides. In the semi-dark, Katy sought to soothe her aching heart as she soaked her body in a steaming shower.

Her mind drifted back skipping over events of the past few years: Rolf at the beach in California, over Damien's Spring Break. *We were flying that old Snoopy kite*, she remembered.

"Give it string, give it more string, Damien. You won't get it up. You're doing it all wrong!" Rolf had observed impatiently from the sidelines.

"Quick, it's faltering... Run, Damien, run... Oh... Ohhh! Damien!" Katy had pled.

Down into the drink it went. *"I told you, it needs more tail!"* Rolf had criticized.

Katy's heart had ached watching eight year old Damien trying to resurrect the errant aero-craft. Damien, so like his father in looks and build; tall, dark-haired and athletic... but so like her in his heart.

Damien. She remembered the day he had brought home that injured, baby sparrow. They fought all afternoon trying to save it, grinding worms with sand and water and placing droppers-full into its gaping, squawking beak until Rolf came home from work.

"What are you doing? He shrieked. "Don't you realize that thing might be infested with lice? It might carry a disease or fungus or GOD-KNOWS-WHAT! And on my table! Get it out! Let nature take its course. You shouldn't interfere with nature."

They ignored Rolf, but despite heroic efforts, their patient succumbed to the death processes conspired against it, and expired soundlessly in its sleep." I'm thankful it wasn't whimpering when it died," Damien had said.

"Yes, at least it was warm and fed, and surrounded by caring hearts," Katy had agreed with him.

"Yeah Mom, we did our best. Maybe Dad was right, it just wasn't meant to be".

"Oh Damien, my baby..." Katy scrubbed her scalp and skin rigorously, but still felt un-atoned.

Later on Katy stepped out to the side door porch from her kitchen, and spied the cat snoozing on a wooden banister, basking in the early afternoon sun. "Well, Mr. Beggar," she cooed. "In the lap of luxury I see."

The creature opened one eye lazily and closed it again. After that, only the swishing of his tail betrayed any sign of life. Katy decided not to disturb him further, and drove her sedan slowly out of the carport and down the driveway as quietly as she could.

On her way to the grocer's, Katy pondered what to do about the cat. She didn't want *any* company, and he was looking like the type of house-guest that could mooch indefinitely.

By the time she parked her car at Haley's Market, she had decided to post a notice on the community bulletin board just inside the entrance:

FOUND
Large, orange, male tabby cat
Vicinity of Molly Court
604-555-3574

After foraging through the store for a few staples and a bit of cat food... *Just in case*, she thought... Katy headed straight home. The checkout clerk had recognized her, but since the accident, he had given up trying to make conversation with Mrs. Steunenberg. It would only lead to an uncomfortable exercise for them both. Everyone in the town of Leone, who knew her, gave Katy a wide berth by mutual consent.

That evening, the cat was gone when Katy checked the side porch. After eating a salad and watching an old black and white movie, she carried her weary bones to bed. She felt a lot older than thirty-two. And wasn't even sure if that *really* was her age, since she hadn't celebrated a birthday the last few years. Rolf hadn't been one for celebrations and she had no family nearby.

That night, she fell again into a rendition of her recurring nightmare: She was in a long, curving hallway, with doors interspersed on either side. She could hear a roaring tiger in pursuit, though she never saw it. Yet, she was sure it was a tiger and not any other type of wildcat. She kept trying doors as she ran down the hall, seeking a way *out*. All of them opened, but only led to small empty rooms with no exits. Finally, exhausted, she arrived at the last door at the very end of the hall. It was locked. It was always locked. Threatening growls were closing in on her from just beyond the last curve she had negotiated.

She woke up terrified. "No, no! It's not real! I'm not really there. It's just a dream, a bad dream." She sat up, hugged her knees to her chest, and began humming her favourite lullaby. Over and over she repeated the refrain in her mind;

The lambs are asleep and baby is too,
God and His angels watch over you...

"Oh, Damien," she murmured. "I'm so, so sorry, my darling."
Then Katy cried pitifully until slumber reclaimed her.

CHAPTER TWO

DESPERADO

The next morning, the supplicant was at it again: "Rrrrreowww! RRRRREEEOOOWWWW!!"

Despite her own despondence, Katy felt sympathy for the poor creature's suffering. She put on a housecoat and opened the side door. "Well, Mr. ..., Mr., what's your name anyway?"

The cat approached the door. "Reow?"

"Garth is it? Yeah, you look like a Garth. Well, Garth, your mistress, or master should be coming to fetch you in a day or two, but in the meantime, I can't have you shattering my solitude, do you hear?"

"Eeow?" The cat seemed to query, cocking his head and looking up at her.

"Hush. I'll be right back with your breakfast." Then over her shoulder she asked through the screen door, "Would you like liver or chicken?"

"Garth" seemed contented with the news of a meal, and leaving the choice to Katy, sat patiently on her porch awaiting his prize. The sun was barely over the horizon and Katy warmed to the stillness about her. She sat on the porch steps and sipped her tea, while Garth lounged beside her for company.

A couple more of days of the same routine, and Katy was almost looking forward to Garth's visits, though she would never have admitted it. She loved peace and quiet, mostly keeping a schedule offset from the rest of the world's rhythm. This was a new experience for her and she was relishing it, despite herself.

Then one morning, the phone rang. Its unfamiliar intrusion

startled her, causing her to drop the design digest she had been absently thumbing through.

"Hello? Yes... Yes, he has been here," she responded. "Well, yes, this afternoon around five would be fine. I can't guarantee he'll be here, but you're welcome to check. He does wander off occasionally, though he seems to be returning with regularity... Eight-seventy-four Appletree Lane."

"Oh," the caller said knowingly. "I'll be there around five-fifteen."

At five twenty a black sports car pulled up in front of the house. Katy watched from behind the blinds as its occupant unfolded his six-foot frame from behind the wheel and headed through the broken gate and up the front walk.

He was trim and well-dressed, but had an air of playfulness. She smiled when she made out his cartoon tie. He looked about thirty-five. *Probably a salesman*, she speculated. When he winced at her unkempt yard, Katy felt a twinge of embarrassment; wishing for that instant, that both she and it were more presentable.

Biting her lower lip, she went out the front door to meet him on the porch. *I certainly don't want him inside.*

"Is he here?" The man inquired brightly, stopping with one foot on the bottom step of her front porch. His warm smile and easy manner challenged Katy's armour.

"Uh, he was a while ago," she said, looking around for the rascal.

"My wife used to take care of the cat. Babied it's actually more like it. I try to keep up with everything, but lately I've been putting in a lot of time at the office. My promotion at Stakles means more hours," the stranger explained absently while rubbing the back of his neck and looking down. "You know how it is," he said, looking back up at Katy and then around for his delinquent pet. He squinted his mischievous green eyes, shading them with his hand, when he looked toward the west and he shrugged sheepishly, "I'm afraid Duffy's been neglected a bit. I try to make it up to him double later, but I guess he decided to secure a back-up source of sustenance, just to be on the safe side."

"Yes, he is a weasel," Katy laughed lightly, noting the cat's name was Duffy.

"We...uh, my wife and I, used to rent this house from the

20

Cramers until three years ago. Now I have a place on Caperro, up five or six blocks further," he said motioning toward the park on the corner. He took a couple of steps back and again looked around for the cat. When he looked back, Katy had come down the stairs and was also looking around for the cat, but she locked eyes with him when he stared right at her. He couldn't help but be drawn into the deep blue pools of hers. They were at once warding off and yet pleading. He wondered at the intensity of them.

After a brief silence, Katy looked away and offered, "We bought this place just about that time. The Cramers must have listed it shortly after you left."

He was mesmerized by her mouth, and the way she enunciated her words, clearly, but with a silky, rose petal voice. He knew he shouldn't stare, but couldn't help himself. She seemed so *vulnerable*.

"You old *skeezix*!" the man exclaimed, suddenly distracted by the cat, as it sashayed around the corner of Katy's house towards them.

"I never let him in, so he shouldn't be too inclined to want to stick around once you've remedied your feeding problems," Katy half-smiled.

Just then, the cat brushed past the man and began purring and weaving around her ankles. Katy giggled involuntarily, and bent down to pick up the cat. "Well, Gar... Duffy, it appears you *do* have a home indeed, and I am sure that Mr., er, uh…"

"Johnson, Garth Johnson," the stranger offered, extending his hand, but deciding to take Duffy off her hands instead, as a handshake would make it impossible for her to hold the tub-o'-lard with only one hand.

Katy blushed at the name coincidence, but never missed a beat, "Mr. Johnson here, will endeavour to take better care of you. So you needn't pester me anymore."

She was scratching his ears, and said this with such affection, that Garth wondered if Duffy would really heed her admonition. His face flushed with her gentle reference to his neglect, and he rubbed his hand on the back of his neck once more before fully taking the cat from Katy. He determined to do better from here-on-out, and said so.

CHAPTER THREE

STRATEGY

Duffy had a mind of his own, and whether or not he understood the terms laid out, he was at Katy's the very next morning having already polished off his dishful of provender at home.

Katy tried to ignore his pleading, but eventually, it got the better of her. She finally decided to give him a saucer of milk, nothing more. But the cat hung around all day, and by the time Garth arrived, Duffy had already convinced Katy to cut him up some sausage. She was sitting on the front steps when Garth pulled up.

"I'm sorry," Garth yelled, entering the still-broken front gate and spotting Duffy on the side porch finishing his victor's spoil. "I rushed home at lunchtime, and put out a package of his favourite tidbits, but I'm afraid, I can't compete with whatever it is you're offering here, Miss...?"

"Katy, Katy Steunenburg," Katy said fidgeting her hands. "I'm sorry too, but I just couldn't bear his pathetic wailing any longer. He wouldn't leave, no matter what I tried. "What if..." She began again, "What if I took Duffy home every time he shows up here and we fed him at your place? Sort of like an incentive reward program," Katy suggested, not sure how else to remedy the situation, and desperate to not let it go any further.

"Hmmm", Garth furrowed his brow and rubbed his cleft chin, then grinned looking from Katy to Duffy and back again. "I hate to impose, but I don't see as I have a choice. Unless..., you'd like a cat? I wouldn't mind giving him to you. He never really was *my* pet and with my wife gone..."

"Oh, no, I couldn't. Really," Katy interrupted hastily. I prefer my solitude and would rather encourage Duffy to make his home with you. I'd be willing to facilitate that program. I'm home all day and, well, if you weren't home, I could still put a dish of food out for him at your place, if that's all right with you?"

And so, it was settled.

Sure enough, the next morning, Duffy was at Katy's door. "Meeeooowww? Meeeooowww?" Katy stuffed Garth's address into her purse, dashed out the door, and scooped up the shameless moocher. "Okay, Duffy, this has gotta work. We can't keep meeting like this!"

Katy easily found Garth's house and the freeze-dried cat food packages that Garth had promised to leave on his front sun-porch near the cat door. She put Duffy down and walked over to his bowl, noticing that he had not even finished what Garth had left in it that morning.

"What? You Sneaky Pete you! Shame on you Duffy!"

Duffy slunk down and crawled a few steps toward her and laid prostrate. Looking for all the world like he knew what *he* was up to and "What was her problem?"

"I guess you prefer my brand of cat food, huh? Well, I'll see if Garth is willing to spring for the Pampercat label. I never should've indulged your senses, you... you weasel!"

Katy left Duffy in her car while she zipped into the market and picked up a few cans of the illicit food. She hoped Garth would understand. *What else can I do?* She reasoned.

Once back at Garth's place, Katy grabbed a can out of the bag with one hand, and Duffy with the other, and headed toward Garth's sun-porch. When she put Duffy down, he sat and watched Katy open the beef Pampercat food. He growled his approval and set out to make short work of the treat. Katy lingered slightly to watch Duffy's delight, but before he was done she got in her car and left, calling Garth at Stakles when she got home, to report the events.

"Well," he laughed, "I never knew I had a gourmet on my hands. It's a good thing I recently got a raise! "Thanks for covering for me again. I hope it won't take much more of this for Duffy to get a sense of where he belongs. How much do I owe you for the food?"

"Not to worry, it was my parting gift to Duffy," Katy replied cheerily.

"Well, at least let me make it up to you. How about... How about dinner? I can pick you up? Or meet you somewhere you if you'd like, and if your husband or boyfriend doesn't mind?"

Katy's throat threatened to close completely. "I don't have a... um, well... o—kay", she acquiesced shrugging, not knowing what else to say.

Garth had chosen a quaint coffee shop that served great pasta and salads. It was quiet and homey and Katy began to relax under his gentle charm. Over a vanilla latte, and at Garth's prompting, she began to share a bit about herself.

"Both of my parents died when I was in high school. They were in their late forties when they adopted me, and never were very healthy. I lived with my older brother until I met my husband Rolf. My brother, Kevin, is now ranching in Argentina. I haven't seen him in about six years. Rolf, my husband, never was too fond of him," she breathed out the last part, her voice barely audible.

Garth was a good listener. He smiled and nodded and made polite comments from time to time, as she described her upbringing. He had the distinct impression, she was single, so he was wondering what had become of Rolf.

After a while, Katy explained quietly, "Rolf and our son, Damien were killed in a car accident almost a year ago. Since then, I... I hardly go out."

"Oh, I'm so sorry," Garth said, putting his cup down. "I know how you feel, Chloe had a brain tumour. It was inoperable. There's nothing we could do but make the best of the time she had left. We spent the first summer in Greece. After that she was too sick to travel or do much of anything. We didn't have any children, just Duffy. He was Chloe's baby. She adored him. I tell ya, sometimes I was jealous of that cat. Not really..., but boy could he ever elicit sympathy and affection from her! Something about cats and women, I sure don't get it," he said, shaking his handsome head. "Like you with Duffy, I mean, I feed him. Sheesh!"

"Do you ever talk to him? Pet him? Scratch his ears?" Katy asked, glad the conversation had moved away from her pain.

"Well, I give him a pat when I come in at night, that is, if he's around. Guess he just likes a lot of attention. Like I told you before, I'm swamped at work and... Oh man! With this promotion, I'm going to be transferred to Vancouver in the Spring... Well, that'll fix his panhandling. At least where you're concerned."

"What kind of work do you do?" Katy asked, genuinely curious.

"I'm a software engineer. Stakles has grown a lot this last year, and I'm training to be the head of a new department at our Vancouver office. It's the break Chloe and I had been waiting for, before starting a family..."

"I'm so sorry about your wife," Katy said, instinctively reaching out to someone who had suffered as much as her.

"I'm dealing with it, Garth smiled sadly. I've been attending meetings with a support group. It's really helped me work through my grief. We meet at St. Andrew's church the first and third Friday of every month. Some great people head up the meetings - really informal you know, but with definite tips. Maybe you should consider going? It might be of interest to you. I don't know," he said staring intently into Katy's eyes, "but it's sure helped me."

"I don't know..." Katy lowered her gaze, her dark lashes caressing her high cheekbones.

"Well, like I said, no pressure. It's real casual..." Garth sat back in his chair and relaxed.

"Can I interest you in dessert?" the waiter interrupted.

This reality check shattered Katy's fragile confidence and she became very quiet. After that, their conversation became stilted and limited to courtesy.

Once they were in the car on the way to Katy's, Garth broke the tension. "Are you warm enough?"

"Yes, thank you", Katy responded automatically.

Then clearing his throat, Garth ventured, "I know it's none of my business, but perhaps you really should consider the grief support meetings. It's surprising what areas of our lives are affected by tragedy. We don't address them unless we're provoked. And unfortunately things don't usually improve on their own..."

"I'm sorry, I'm not interested," Katy asserted.

"Well, maybe another time."

"Yes, maybe…"

But he knew she didn't mean it. Why did it matter so much to him he wondered.

Then after a long silence, Garth spoke up brightly, "My wife was a very organized person. She knew where everything was. You know what I mean? I mean her cupboards were *alphabetized*! Not me. I can't find a thing. Never plan ahead. Don't even own a calendar."

What's that got to do with anything,? Katy wondered to herself.

"Yeah, I just wing it. Works for me… Spontaneity. Don't you agree?" Garth cast a sideways glance in her direction. Before she looked at him, he focused his eyes squarely on the road again.

"I — don't know…" Katy stammered.

"Sure! No commitments, no obligations, just shmoozin' along life's track. Takin' things as they come along…"

"I guess."

Garth continued, "See, that's what I mean. No absolutes. Never nail anything down."

"Well, you have a job, don't you? Obligations? Bills? Duffy?" Katy challenged him.

"Yeah, I guess I do play the game a bit. Not like you…"

"I have responsibilities," Katy responded defensively.

"Ah, but do you make commitments?" Garth asked raising one eyebrow, reminding her of a beloved, elderly professor she had once.

"Well, sure."

"Like maybe attending one meeting?"

"Garth, please," she pleaded flatly.

"Really, I'd go with you…" he said, ignoring her obvious discomfort, "…hold your hand if you want. Just one meeting; Just try *one*."

Looking down demurely, Katy could feel his good-natured grin across the seat, and hated to look at him, feeling herself weakening.

Just then, Garth eased his car in front of Katy's house.

When Katy finally did look at him, his face was serious. She felt captivated by his gaze. She read the compassion with which he was imploring her. Felt he really cared. Cared if she withered away; if she was hopelessly lost…

"O—kay." She said, breaking the trance, "But I'm not going to *say* anything."

"That's okay. Really. You'll see. It'll be good."

27

CHAPTER FOUR

FRIENDSHIP

Oh why did I let Garth talk me into this meeting? I'm not going to air my life in front of a bunch of strangers. What do they know about what I've been through? They're situations are probably all 'clean' ones. No murder/suicides in their closets I'll wager. Well, they'll not have my grief to pander about town. I've got nothing to say to them. I'll just listen. Maybe I'll learn a trick to get rid of my nightmares. I'd be content with that.

And with that mindset, Katy rose to answer the doorbell.

"Hi Garth," she began, "You know, you really didn't have to come get me. I would've found it on my own," Katy remarked getting into Garth's car.

"Well, I was afraid you'd back out. Besides, it helps to have a friend along the first time one goes to a new place, even if it's just for a 'Tupperware™ party'."

Katy laughed in spite of herself. This was not going to be anything *like* a Tupperware party, and they both knew it. *Hopefully everyone will just act civilized, it'll be over quickly, and I'll never attend another one*, Kathy thought to herself.

The meeting was conducted informally. Everyone was congenial and laid back. And once it was apparent that there was going to be no prying, Katy relaxed as best she could.

The guest speaker was a tall, white-haired pastor, with large silver-rimmed glasses. He gently outlined the basic steps of grieving: shock, anger, bargaining, denial, withdrawal, and finally acceptance. He spoke about the different means by which individuals make peace with their sorrow.

"Some people find that talking their concerns out, perhaps even with a professional counselor, or reading books on the subject, to be helpful. Others prefer to initiate private rituals to commemorate the significance of their loved ones' lives."

He then asked for input from the group. An older, dignified, burgundy-haired woman in a raspberry coloured pant-suit, said that she had written a private biography about her husband after his death. She had glued into it keepsakes and documents of their shared experiences: airline ticket stubs, theatre programs, photographs... even his scrawled notes to her. She seemed to be a veteran member of the group. *Almost unaffected at all*, Katy noted. *She's quite 'together' and supportive of the others.*

A young woman who had lost her infant son at birth, quietly shared how she had given her baby a name and attributed a personality to him, based on her impressions of him in the womb. She had stitched a poem that she had written for him, had it framed, and hung it in her bedroom. She had also found great solace in being able to talk to others about her son. What might have been. How he must have been especially needed in heaven — though she found few friends or family members who understood why she still found it necessary, or would even want to talk about him any more. Even her husband had 'moved on', so she was grateful for the support group letting her 'vent her spleen'.

Garth surprised Katy by standing up and saying that he had maintained his wife's flower garden and tried to look after her cat as she would have wanted him to. He said he felt her approval and this gave him peace.

The remainder of the meeting was comprised of casual conversations over refreshments. Some members were discussing aspects of their loved one's passing, others, just general topics. One woman was asking how to find a good, honest mechanic. Her husband had always taken care of things and now she was having to form a list of reliable handymen, to get jobs done. Katy was impressed with the woman's level headed approach at solving her problems, rather than capitulating to them. Katy wished she had that strength. She had no reservoir to draw on. Not even a real "want to"; or, not enough of one, anyway.

When the meeting was finished, Garth drove Katy home, and respecting her silence, said nothing unnecessary during the drive.

Only that he'd like her to consider going to the next meeting, and that he'd call to see if he could pick her up.

"I'll let you know," was all she could manage.

CHAPTER FIVE

CONFESSION

Because of what was said at the meeting, Katy worked up the courage over the next few days to venture into Damien's room. She had a new yearning to try and make a truce with her pain. To find "peace in acceptance" and instinctively she felt that Damien's room held the key. She took a deep breath, and opened the door slowly. Walking in, as if through water over her head, she gingerly went through his closet and drawers, remembering items as she touched them lovingly: his jacket, his skateboard, his Ipod™ , his sneakers...

Going through Rolf 's articles had been relatively easy. She still had a lot of anger then. She had thrown out almost everything personal, and sent the rest of his things to the handicapped society - whatever she had deemed would help improve the lot of some poor soul. Thankfully, her friend Cheryl was still around to help her get through that time.

But Damien's things were sacred. Even now, she did not move them, except to look at them and replace them exactly where they had been. She didn't know what she was looking for… maybe nothing in particular, just a collection of her thoughts, the mastery of her savage pain, some rationale for what had happened.

As she opened Damien's desk drawer, she saw his school binder, and as she leafed through it, she came across an essay they had worked on together the month before the crash, entitled:

Wild Cats - Siberian Tigers.

She read:

The Siberian Tiger is the largest of all tigers. Tigers generally have two to six cubs, though less than half survive to maturity. Such is the harshness of their surroundings; both predators and elements of nature. The female tiger is very protective of her young, but will leave them increasingly on their own in order to develop their survival skills. The young tiger learns to hunt by modeling its mother's actions. The mother will maim a potential prey, disabling it in order for the cubs to experience the kill.

Female tigers are territorial, and will not even permit adult male tigers in their domain except for breeding. A mother's cubs grow apart from their dependence on her, until even they are unwelcome in her terrain...

Damien, I never pushed you away... even as you got older. We did lots of things together. You were my life! Sure, you were growing up and finding your own way, but I always wanted you around. I only tried to protect you from your Dad, his influence.

You were never like him, anyway. You were sensitive, and sweet... Oh my baby, I miss you so much! Salty droplets spilled down her cheeks.

Then, blinking, she read: **Siberian Tigers are prized for their...** Katy's vision blurred completely.

You were prized. I will preserve your memory. I'll have a chest made. A keepsake chest. It will protect and guard your cherished treasures. My treasures now. The rest of your things, your furniture, and clothes, they should have a new owner. Someone who needs them. I saw a sign on the bulletin board at the store the other day. There was a family who lost everything in a fire. Yes! They may have a son that needs warmth and a bed. He shall have them. For you will always stay warm in my heart, Love.

Almost two weeks passed and Duffy never returned to Katy's. *Guess he finally got what he wanted,* she surmised. *He sure knows how to fend for himself. Just like a young tiger coming into his own. Hmmm...* Katy mused. *Just like Damien.*

Maybe I should take the left over cans of cat food to Garth's. I'll just leave them on his sun-porch by the emergency stock. He probably won't even notice. I'll be gone before he gets off work...

Katy changed her clothes before going out and ran a brush through her hair. She decided to put some colour onto her cheeks and lips, *just a bit*, she thought, feeling celebratory over her commemorative ideas: she had chosen a chest design at the local artisans and had arranged to have it made. Then she drove over to Garth and Duffy's.

"I might've known I'd find you here lounging and catching some rays!" Katy laughed shaking her head. "Forgot your old friend already, haven't you?" Duffy's eyes were closed, and he peeked only slightly, eyeing Katy without much interest. But when she emptied her bag by the other cans of Pamper cat food on the porch, Duffy stretched and yawned. Then nonchalantly meandered over to Katy and gave her his best "MEEOOWW" while rubbing up against her leg.

"No way! You've probably already eaten twice today. Look at the size of you! What a tub-o-lard!" she exclaimed. But she sat down beside the poor creature and began to scratch his fluffy head, sympathizing that Garth probably didn't have the time. Duffy curled onto her lap and purred so contentedly, that Katy couldn't bring herself to stop. She petted and preened Duffy, and let the sun soak into her bones. *It is a lazy afternoon after all*, she reasoned, closing her eyes and humming her lullaby and day-dreaming as she lavished her affection on the wallowing cat.

Only when she heard Garth's car pull up did she extricate herself from the reverie, and how! Poor Duffy was quickly dusted aside and Katy was halfway to her car before Garth was out of his.

"Hey! What's goin' on?" he beamed.

"Oh, I was just leaving, she stammered. I brought some left-over cat food by. I figured you could make use of it."

"How are you? I was going to call you tonight and see if we are still on for tomorrow."

"Tomorrow? Well, of course. Sorry, I've gotta run." And with that, she jumped into her car and was gone, before Garth could press her any further.

"What a goof," she reprimanded herself once she was down the road. "Don't even know how to act around a man anymore. What's the big deal? Now he'll think I'm looney for sure!"

The next night, Garth phoned at five o'clock to say that he'd be over to pick her up at seven. "I'm just heading home from work, and wanted to verify a pickup time." When she agreed, he politely ended the conversation and hung up.

"Well, no chance of his being interested in me, except as a social project. Why do I even care?" she berated herself. "I can't have a normal life, be average. I've lived through hell and it's tainted me forever, I'm untouchable... in a class by myself," Katy muttered.

The next support group meeting was not as intense for Katy. There wasn't a guest speaker, only a group discussion and the topics seemed relatively "safe". The facilitator opened with a prayer, one that he read: it reflected the cry of a tragedy survivor. A cry for sense, a cry for peace, a cry for wholeness and an expression of gratitude to a God who knows all, cares deeply and who will make everything right. This thought comforted Katy, and she determined to retain it.

After that, a middle-aged man that she hadn't seen at the previous meeting spoke up. "As you all know, our daughter was murdered seven years ago. It took a long time to find out who did it, though we'll never know his reasons. After a six-year investigation and grueling trial, her killer was sentenced last week. My wife and I feel like we can finally begin the healing process. It has taken all our strength to cope with the legal proceedings..."

Oh, Katy thought, *what a heart-ache... to have your child murdered by a stranger. To not even know who did it or why... At least I know.*

After that, the conversation revolved around: how to survive the holidays; practical ideas on how to cope without a spouse's help in running a household; and networking with friends, relatives and professionals with expertise in particular areas.

It was also apparent to Katy, that these people considered each other valid sources of assistance. There were many solutions found within the group, and more than one hug shared. They were almost a family unto themselves, bonded closer than many blood relatives she had known.

Katy was silent most of the evening, but made mental notes, and even sent up a silent prayer at one point. Garth would catch her eye from time to time and she couldn't help but return his encouraging smiles. She was surprised the time had passed so quickly, when it was over. She helped clean up the refreshments while Garth assisted with stacking the chairs. She stopped and smiled at the children's Sunday-school colouring pictures and

featured on the walls,

came across a framed poster of Jesus laughing. She'd never thought of **Him** that way, laughing!

As they were leaving, Garth put his arm around her in a comforting gesture, and held out an open umbrella that he had thought to bring along to protect her from a pelting rain that had started as they walked to the parking lot.

Once they were in the car he asked brightly: "So, what are you doing for Thanksgiving?"

"When is it?" Katy asked absently stuffing the meeting handout into her purse.

"Two weeks from next Monday."

"Oh," she breathed out.

"So, what are your plans?" Garth asked, realizing she probably had not celebrated any holidays since the accident.

"I haven't any."

"Well, then, maybe we could..." he started, as he drove the car into traffic.

"No, *we*, I, I couldn't..."

"C'mon, you need to get out more. It'll do you good. I can prepare the whole thing. I've gotten to be quite a chef the last couple of years."

"No, you don't understand, Katy whispered huskily. "Damien and Rolf died on Thanksgiving. Actually, the Friday night before..."

Katy began to weep softly, and Garth slowed the car down, before pulling over and stopping.

"I'm sorry," he said tenderly. "I didn't realize..."

"It was supposed to be a father/son fishing trip." Katy sniffed, looking down at her hands. "Rolf finally had some time off work. He'd been working six days a week for months. Damien was so looking forward to it. He so wanted to do manly things with his Dad."

"Rolf and I had an argument that morning," Katy confessed. "He didn't want to cut their trip short to come back in time for a traditional turkey dinner on Monday. He figured if they were driving all that way, they should maximize their stay. He was looking forward to his time off, and spending it in a way that suited him."

She continued, almost unable to stop once she started, "I was angry at his always trying to control the entire family with his selfish whims. He never did what anyone else wanted."

Katy tilted her head back, and ran her fingers through her hair, lifting it from behind and letting it fall with a sigh. "Even if I let him know what I wanted to do, he'd end up ridiculing my wishes and ramming his ideas through. Despite my awareness of this fact, I was never able to dissuade him. No matter how much I protested, he always ended up getting his way."

She shook her head, still trying to comprehend the man she'd married this long after his death.

Garth nodded compassionately, but didn't interrupt her.

"That morning, I was trying once again to change his mind. It was set in concrete. All he bared was his 'poor me' attitude. He was feeling so sorry for himself and all the overtime he'd put in, that he refused to consider my suggestion.

"I told him that I didn't know why I stuck around. That he never was a husband to me, or even much of a father to Damien. I told him that I'd had it. That I was thinking about leaving him, and that I might not be there when he got back. He said that was fine with him, but not to even *think* about getting custody of Damien; that he would never allow me to have him, never!" And she began sobbing again.

"Oh, Katy." Garth turned off the engine, and with heavy rain pouring down on the windshield, the wipers ticked away the minutes of silence between them.

Katy pulled a tissue from her purse and began wiping her eyes and blew her nose.

"Garth, I've never told anyone this," she said turning to look into his eyes, "But I, I think Rolf was committing suicide when the car went off the road into the ravine. That he purposefully took Damien with him to hurt me... the ultimate control stunt. He'd been angry and depressed for years. He hated his job. I think he even resented me."

Garth reached over and put his hand on hers, but he didn't say anything. His wise, tender eyes expressed his deep sympathy for her pain.

She continued, "The coroner's report indicated no reason for the car going off the road," she said looking away. Through her tears, she stared unseeing out the rain-blurred windshield.

"Rolf had threatened suicide many times. I always thought it was a desperate attempt at controlling me. Keeping me feeling sorry for him, keeping me giving in… I never thought he'd really do it."

Katy took a deep breath, and blew it out forcefully, realizing with it, that the dam had finally broken within her. She looked again at Garth. While keeping his gaze fixed, he squeezed her hand between both of his.

She continued in low tones with her confessional: "As he left with Damien that morning to drive him to school, I casually asked him when they would be back. Damien had no inkling of the chasm that had developed between Rolf and me. When Rolf said late Monday night, I just stared at him: his rock face; his cold eyes. Right then I had a premonition that something was horribly wrong… that I should not let my son go with this, mad man. Yet I could think of nothing to say to bar their leaving. Damien really wanted to go with his father. What could I say? Oh, I'll never forgive myself!"

Garth jumped in, "But, Katy, how could you know? You couldn't keep Damien from his father indefinitely. You didn't do anything wrong! Rolf did. Don't let him continue to control you with this. Please, listen to me. You've got to let it go."

Garth slipped his arm around her, and Katy collapsed into his broad chest. The dam burst completely and Katy was crying from her depths now; the gut-wrenching wail of an empty-armed mother, a woman drowning in guilt.

"There, there, it's okay," Garth soothed, stroking her hair. "Just let it go. You've suffered so much. You can't carry this alone. I'm here for you. Katy, Katy, shhhh..."

Katy felt herself begin to truly 'let go' from somewhere deep inside. Like a frozen river breaking up during spring thaw, her anxieties were beginning to melt in Garth's warm embrace. She could've stayed there forever, but eventually he smoothed her hair and released her gently. He drove slowly to her house, holding her hand and all the while consoling her with comforting words. When they pulled in the driveway beside her house, Garth turned off the engine and they sat a long time in silence.

When Katy got out of the car, Garth walked her to the door and elicited a promise from her that she would be okay.

Feeling ashamed and confused, she nodded and smiled wanly. Her composure, however was tenuous, and once inside, when she was sure he was gone, Katy yielded to the wild, pent up pressure in her chest and a fresh batch of tears were released.

Flinging herself on her bed she wailed an unearthly groan. She cried for Damien, for Rolf, for herself, for the shame and the searing pain. She also cried for the feelings stirring inside herself for Garth. She had been numb for so long, that her senses now felt raw and exposed, while at the same time salved and comforted. She reasoned that he was only being compassionate, and not her knight.

She would never have a knight. Never...

CHAPTER SIX

RITUALS

Saturday morning the phone rang. Katy was still deep in the clutches of the netherworld. She never saw them but this time there was an entire pack of tigers chasing her relentlessly. Down, down the hallway. She kept running, trying to find a way out, or wanting the ordeal at least to have it end, even if it meant being devoured after all.

"Hello?" she answered the telephone groggily.

"Katy? It's Garth. Are you okay?"

"Um, yeah, uh-huh..."

"Did I wake you? I'm sorry. I'll call back later."

"No, it's okay. I should be getting up. What time is it?"

"It's about nine-thirty. I was going to call earlier, but waited as long as I could, in case you were still asleep. Gosh, I'm sorry. Anyway, as long as you're up, how'd you like to go out for a nice hearty breakfast, my treat?"

"All right," Katy heard herself say. "When?"

"How about, I pick you up in an hour?"

"Uh, actually, no," she said shaking her head awake. "I shouldn't. I can't. I'm sorry. Thank you for calling. I'm fine. Really." And she hung up, quickly sinking into a pit of brooding.

Garth didn't call back.

Katy went to the furniture shop to pick up the chest the following Monday. It wouldn't fit in her trunk as expected, so the manager said he'd have it delivered on Tuesday. Katy waited all day for the truck, but the chest didn't arrive until six o'clock that evening.

During the day, she sorted through Damien's things and had them all ready for their final resting place. She was thankful for something to do. It kept her mind off Garth and what to do about him, or if anything even *needed* doing.

She telephoned the relief shelter and arranged to have Damien's furniture picked up on Thursday. She felt good to have made such positive strides.

That night, after eating a muffin with jam, Katy began putting Damien's things in the chest, and spoke to him as she did: "I used to love watching you play baseball, you were such a good sport. Remember the day at Spence Park when you hit that 'homer'? I was so proud... you were everything good and perfect. Even when you were mad at me, like the time I wouldn't let you miss school to go to Disneyland with Ty's family. You only felt bad because your friend would have to tough it alone with his two sisters..."

"Your jacket still smells like the great outdoors... "I will always keep your prized skateboard and your Gameboy™... Your dinosaur models and your stickers; you'll never outgrow them in my mind."

Katy added the contents of Damien's 'baby box' including his blankie, silver cup and the hand-knit outfits she had made him. She smelled them and caressed them gently, winding the ribbons around her finger. "What a beautiful baby you were! Even the nurses at the hospital said so. You were even-tempered and sweet as pie..."

Later, Katy curled up in bed that night, nursing a peaceful satisfaction. There was no dreaming, only a calm tranquility. She slept deep and snug and long.

CHAPTER SEVEN

REFRESH

The following Saturday morning Katy was in the kitchen stirring a pot of oatmeal when she heard a strange, low moaning sound outdoors on the side porch. Peeking out the window, she exclaimed, "Duffy! What are you doing here?"

From what she could see, he looked injured.

"What, what happened to you?" she shrieked, quickly opening the door. There sat Duffy looking very forlorn and all chewed up. He had blood on his ears and face and was limping with his head hung down sideways toward her. She gently picked him up and brought him inside, cooing, "You poor baby. Oh, what happened?"

She warmed up some milk and while he drank it, she called Garth. "...he seems to have been in some sort of fight. No, I don't think it's life-threatening. Poor Duffy. He must've crossed into some other cat's domain... No, I'll bring him over after breakfast. I want to. Yes, he'll be fine 'til then." She hung up the phone and sighed.

When Katy pulled up to Garth's, his car was in the driveway with buckets, sponges and a garden hose surrounding it. He was a few houses up the street with his head under the hood of an older red sports car. A blonde "bombshell" was leaning towards him under it too.

She seems a tad overdressed for a casual weekend, Katy observed. *Make that underdressed...*

When Garth spotted her, he waved gallantly, and headed home. Katy waved back, and waited by Garth's car, cradling the injured patient in a towel. Duffy made no attempt to free himself from

Katy, so she continued holding him and crooned softly: It's okay Duffers, you'll soon be ensconced in the warmth of your own kingdom again. You shouldn't have ventured from home. It's safer in your own environ..."

Garth approached with the woman not far behind. "Katy, hi!" And as the bombshell approached from behind him, "Uh, this is Susan. We were trying to figure out her carburetor."

Maybe you were, thought Katy. *This woman was showing more than a little cleavage, and seemed intent on holding Garth's attention.*

"Oh, hi Kathy." The woman chattered on, "I just can't function without my wheels. Garth is such a gentleman. I don't know what I'd do without his expertise."

Female tigers are territorial. Katy dismissed the thought and said "Hello", nodding politely.

"Now how's our philanderer?" Garth said closing in on the patient.

Which one? Katy mused to herself, stifling a smile.

"I guess we'll have to pay a visit to the vet," Garth exclaimed after a cursory examination of Duffy's injuries. "Don't suppose you'd come along?" Garth said almost imploringly to Katy. "You know, for moral support?"

"No, I can't," said Katy, "I have an appointment."

"At nine a.m. on a Saturday?" Garth asked.

"Yes", said Katy, not offering any explanation.

"Well, I'm free," offered Susan.

"Oh, that's okay," said Garth, dismissing her offer while still looking at Katy. "No telling how long it will take. I don't know if the animal clinic is even open this early. Guess we're on our own Old Buddy," he said, lifting Duffy out of his cocoon. Duffy went to jump down but Garth held him firm, and placed him in his car from the passenger side.

He cleared the buckets away from in front of his vehicle, while Katy pulled the hose out of his way. "Well, we're off ladies," Garth said as he opened the driver's door. "See you next Friday Katy?"

"Yes, next Friday." Katy responded a little too enthusiastically, mostly because of the threatening predator.

"Yeah, bye," the bombshell fizzled, and shuffled away.

Katy drove to the strip mall out on the highway to get her hair cut at 'Super-Snips'. "See, I really did have an appointment," she said out loud, pulling into a parking spot. "Sort of." Although the discount studio didn't make appointments, and she would've preferred going to her old salon in town... but she hadn't been there since before disaster struck. It was too familiar... too awkward.

"Let's see now, you want your front cut into bangs, the back trimmed and a super conditioning treatment. Tsk, tsk. Yes... You've been neglecting your hair, haven't you?" the saucy hair dresser observed, shaking her cornrow braided head while chomping her gum and lifting a strand of Katy's lacklustre, golden locks. "My, my, so many split ends. Sure you don't want a whole new look? I could style this into a nouveau short cut."

"No short-cuts for me," Katy smiled and enjoyed the pampering, styling process, despite her attendant's mannerisms. The girl was obviously preoccupied with the young man seated in the chair next to hers and Katy was thankful that she kept her comments at a 'professional' level.

The young man was mouthing macho bravado to *his* stylist while she added more spiking gel to his locks. This evened up his look, but didn't improve it in Katy's opinion, though she could see that *her* hair dresser was duly impressed.

Magnetism. There's no accounting for it. It's just animalistic. Katy mused. Then she began thinking about Garth.

He's good looking to be sure. Not too flashy, but a nice dresser... not too casual, not 'too much'. Wonder where he works out? Working in an office all day, doesn't lend itself to his type of physique. Hmmm...

Her stylist couldn't help playing with Katy's hair just a little and even Katy had to admit the moderately updated style *was* becoming. She left the salon feeling elated and emancipated... as if more than just some of her hair had been cut off.

She sucked in the fresh fall air hungrily and walked around the plaza window-shopping and day-dreaming before buying some flowers to take home.

CHAPTER EIGHT

LOVINGKINDNESS

On Friday afternoon, Garth called to see if Katy would like to go out for supper before the meeting.

"Sure, that'd be great!" Katy said, blushing at her over eager tone.

"Great, I'll get off early and pick you up at 5:00, okay?"

"That'll be fine," Katy said flatly, back-peddling.

When Garth picked her up he gave her a simple caring hug at her door and asked if she was 'doin' okay'. Katy didn't read anything into it, but the compassion of a friend. Thinking of Garth merely as a friend, helped her to lighten up a little.

"Yes, thanks. I'm much better," Katy said smiling.

Garth drove to an Italian restaurant on Lakeshore Drive situated on the way to the meeting. The owner seated them at a checker-clothed table with the 'besta viewa in the house'. It was still early and there were no other patrons, so they privately enjoyed the restaurant's ambience and the lake's October solitude.

A fireplace crackled at one end of the room, and a miniature, frosted glass sculpture on their table held a single tea light. In its soft light, Garth murmured, "You look different, Katy."

"Oh, I had my hair trimmed." she demurred.

"It's, not just that. You seem more settled. More at peace. I was worried about you after last week," he said, passing her a basket of foccacia bread the waiter had left.

"I'm fine... working through a few things, actually. I went into Damien's room for the first time last month," Katy said, breaking a piece off her bread. She held both pieces absently, reflecting on the experience. "It was good. Good to remember. I even planned my own 'memorial' - a keepsake chest. I put Damien's mementos into it. The rest of his stuff, you know, clothes, furniture..., went to a destitute family."

"Good for you, Katy. I'm proud of you. I know our last session was hard on you and our conversation on the way home..."

"It's okay," she interrupted him. "I needed to get it out. I've had no one to talk to. My best friend moved to California shortly after the wreck. Since then, I've been going it alone. Actually, I haven't *gone* anywhere, just spun out's more like it."

"You don't work?"

"No. I used to be a decorator for Artisans downtown, but I gave it up. I have the insurance money, and my needs are few. I just didn't have the heart to face anyone anymore."

Garth was moved by her gentle voice and the sweet way she emphasized her s's.

He glanced out the window and they both were captivated by the variegated pinks of an exquisite sunset and sat in silence for a moment. Muted, tenor opera music was providing a seductive backdrop to this moment of wonder. Suddenly Garth's logic kicked in. "Insurance money? So your agency didn't feel it was a suicide, did they?"

"No, they ruled it an accident. I had no proof. No note... just my own feelings screaming at me. Rolf was a good driver. He prided himself on his incisive handling of a vehicle."

She said the word 'incisive', remembering how Rolf had used it in the same context. "The conditions were fair", she continued. "And the vehicle inspection revealed no flaws. There were no skid marks on the road, as if he had tried to stop. No other vehicles were involved. Witnesses said the car just drove off the road."

Garth looked pensive. "Well, you never know... You shouldn't beat yourself up about this. There could be other explanations..."

"I suppose. But none seem plausible to me. He had no alcohol in his bloodstream. They did an autopsy and his heart was fine. Everything was fine."

Tears threatened again, and Garth astutely redirected the conversation. "Duffy is on the mend. The vet said he's lucky. No permanent damage; except his ear looks a little weird now. Oh well, it's a small price to pay for ardour - though I'm sure Duffy's will be cooled for a while. He sticks pretty close to home. It's like we're buddies now. I try to make a point of petting him every day and he usually sacks out on the couch if I'm watching a game at night."

Katy smiled and looked out the window again. The lights from the homes on the other side of the lake were becoming more visible as the sky darkened. She imagined families bustling inside them, observing their domestic evening rituals. Mothers making suppers, fathers reading newspapers or coming in the door with their sons from hockey practice. Daughters chatting on the phone with their friends who they'd just seen all day at school...

It was another world. One she envied.

Turning back to Garth she said. "Thank you for tonight. It's nice not to be eating alone for a change."

Just then the waiter came with their lasagna and removed their salad plates. Katy closed her eyes and recited in her mind a grace she'd learned as child: *Good food, and hearth and home, we thank thee Lord for each and every one.* When she looked up, Garth was smiling at her. The rest of their conversation was natural and pleasant.

The speaker that night was a psychologist, Dr. Layel Raina, who specialized in post-traumatic stress. She was warm and friendly and spoke in lay terms about the evolution of emotions following a tragedy. She gave practical advice about diet, exercise, and pacing oneself. Then she mentioned the benefits of professional grief counseling.

Katy felt that Dr. Raina articulated exactly what she had been feeling and considered making an appointment to see her, wondering if it *really* could make a difference.

On the way home Garth chatted about his work, his upcoming transfer at the beginning of March, and then he invited Katy to dinner on Monday for Thanksgiving, again. "So, do you feel up to my cooking?"

"I should be cooking for you", she responded. "You've taken me out twice already."

"My pleasure," he interrupted. "Besides, that's what friends are for! You'll get your turn."

"What about your family?" Katy asked, noting his reference to a future meal at her place.

"Oh, just a few married nieces and a nephew in Vancouver. My sister and her husband are in Egypt. He's an economist, contracted to a university there for another six years. Then he retires. Their kids would include me in their festivities, but I'd just as soon spend a quiet day at home: just me and Duffy, and you... if you're game?"

"Speaking of games," Katy interjected, "does that dinner include a football game by any chance?"

"Well, of course! It's as traditional as turkey!"

"Who's playing? I haven't seen a game since Damien and I used to watch them." "Toronto and Montreal ".

"Sounds great! M-maybe I could bring dessert?"

"Great, it's settled then!"

CHAPTER NINE

GIVING THANKS

On Monday afternoon, the game was filled with twists and turns, keeping Garth and Katy glued to the set. Afterwards, they ate a reasonable facsimile of the traditional Thanksgiving feast being enjoyed in homes across Canada. When Garth said grace, Katy was moved by how he spoke to God as a loving, heavenly father. She basked in the warm glow of this comforting thought.

"Garth, you *are* a good cook! I've never had such scrumptious potatoes," Katy exclaimed.

"It's the whipping cream, my own specialty."

By the time they finished dessert and cleaned up, the sun had lowered beyond the horizon.

Garth leaned over the sink and looked dejectedly out the window. "Well, I was going to invite you for a walk, but it's gotten pretty dark out there."

"It's not so bad. I wouldn't mind some fresh air", Katy said, dishing some turkey scraps into Duffy's personalized bowl. "I wouldn't go out alone at night, but I feel quite safe with you." And she acknowledged in her heart how good 'safe' felt.

The sky was clear and the heavenly bodies were crisply defined. The moon was nearly full and seemed to smile on their pathway as Garth directed Katy across a vast playing field between the streetlights of his neighborhood and a well-lit high-school track. A few die-hard fitness freaks were jogging around it.

As they sat on the bleachers, Katy began to reminisce about Damien and his love of sports... "He wasn't very accomplished, but he loved a good game. He tried out for everything: basketball, baseball, hockey... "He used to play table hockey with me. I even won once in a while!" she giggled, recalling.

"His father wasn't into sports much except fishing and bow hunting. Damien didn't seem to mind tagging along with his friends and their fathers to practice sessions though."

She was quiet for a moment, and they both sat comfortably, with their own bitter-sweet thoughts.

"He sounds like a good kid, Katy," Garth said, breaking the silence.

Hanging her head slightly, she nodded, then shivered and pulled her woolen anorak around her neck more snugly.

"What sports are you into, Garth?" she said turning her face toward him.

"Just about everything" he said, shuffling his feet. Though as a participant, I've mostly been sticking to squash lately. It's hard to fit athletics into my schedule, except for the gym three times a week." He stood up with his hands in his pockets and faced her. "I enjoy watching televised events. The coverage is better than live anyway.

"Hey, we should get you home and warmed up", he said noting her shivering. "How about some tea?"

"Yeah, I guess I am getting cold, but this was nice. Perfect. Thank you for a great day. Everything Thanksgiving should be!" Katy was fighting her emotions as they walked back: thinking about Rolf and Damien, and organizing her thoughts given the events of the last few weeks. Wondering how Garth really felt about her. Wondering how she really felt about him. *Maybe I'm just so hard up for attention, I'd imagine that anyone cared romantically for me.* By the time they approached his front door, she blurted out quickly: "I guess I should be getting home. You have to work tomorrow."

"That's okay, I can handle a late night now and then." Garth said easily. "C'mon, I'll make you a special hot toddy."

"No, it's late. I'm tired. I'll just get my purse and head home."

Garth opened the door for her and threw up his hands. As she brushed past him, Katy wanted to fling herself into his arms, but instead, strode to her purse and scooping it up, gave Duffy a pat goodbye and slipped out the door. Garth was still standing in the doorway not having said another word.

"Katy, Katy, Katy," she castigated herself out loud on the drive home. *"He doesn't care about you. You're just a casualty he encountered along the way. A wounded soldier from the same battle he survived. Your camaraderie is based on nothing more than a common foe: Death. That, and a cat named Duffy."*

Once home, Katy fell into a confused sleep. This time the tiger was visible. It was toying with her. Not killing her outright, but taunting her, threatening her. She vacillated between cowering and trying to fight back. Seemingly equal in strength, they were at a stalemate. Neither side backing down.

CHAPTER TEN

BREAKTHROUGH

Dr. Raina's receptionist showed Katy into her office and said that the doctor would be with her shortly. The room was pleasant and comfortable. It was tastefully decorated in off-white, sea-green and slate blue. There were fresh daisies in a square crystal vase on the credenza and a picture of Dr. Raina's family on the wall. Katy smiled at the littlest boy's freckles and missing front teeth. He reminded her of Damien. Not in looks, but in spirit somehow.

She was startled to realize that Dr. Raina had entered the room and was standing next to her.

"Hello Katy," she said, extending her right hand. "How are you? I'm glad you wanted to see me. I'm sure that together we can uncover some keys that will help you rebuild your life."

"Oh hi, I was admiring your family", Katy said, shaking the doctor's hand. Such a handsome crew.

"Yes, they are quite a crew. Thank you," Dr. Raina said, smiling as she walked across the room to the other side of her desk.

"Please sit down," she said this, motioning to a cozy, green arm chair opposite hers. "Did you have any trouble finding our offices?"

"No, I'm familiar with Vancouver. I used to work downtown. Before..." She looked down, suddenly fearing this was going to be more difficult than she thought.

"Good, then. Now, how can I help you?" Dr. Raina asked pleasantly.

The question surprised Katy. She assumed the doctor would somehow automatically know what was wrong with her and how to fix it. But of course she *must* verbalize her problem before they could find a solution.

Mustering her resolve, Katy began, "Well, a year ago, my husband Rolf and my son Damien, he was eleven then, were killed in a car crash."

Dr. Raina nodded sympathetically.

"Rolf and I weren't exactly getting along when it happened. In fact, I had threatened to leave him that morning. He swore I'd never get Damien, and that he'd fight me for him. Damien never knew any of this, and was really looking forward to a weekend away with his dad. Rolf normally didn't spend much time with him. My husband was in his own little world. He was very selfish and seldom did anything that didn't suit his purposes exclusively. But this fishing trip was something *he* really wanted, and he was willing to include Damien. My son wanted to be closer to his dad, so I let him go. It was against my better judgment after our argument, but I had no *real* reason to object... none but my own foreboding. Rolf looked so... menacing when they pulled out of the driveway that morning." She shuddered involuntarily, suddenly feeling out of breath.

Katy hesitated.

"Yes, go on..." Dr. Raina encouraged.

Katy slowly relayed her suspicions and when she was through, she was relieved to have the awful truth out. She hoped she'd never have to let it see the light of day again.

Dr. Raina, who had listened quietly and nodded encouragingly the entire time, asked: "How've you been sleeping?"

Katy told her about her nightmares.

Then Dr. Raina said, "Guilt is a master tormentor. Even if it's irrational, it can govern our lives, taking a larger and larger part of us into captivity. Some people end up consumed by it. We must afford ourselves the same courtesy we would anyone else. A fair hearing, some human compassion and understanding, time for reflection, and then, forgiveness. Grief is a natural process that will lead us to resolution, provided it isn't hampered by excess baggage, such as guilt."

Katy nodded. "I can see that".

Dr. Raina stretched back in her chair and smiled. "We're running out of time today, but I've got a questionnaire that I'd like you to fill out for our next session. It will help us pinpoint the source of your pain and its tag places. Then we'll work on it together."

After agreeing to attend another session, Katy left feeling more like herself than she had since the accident.

No, before that, she thought. *Since before I met Rolf.* "Please God, she prayed while driving home, let me really be on the mend. Let these sessions with Dr. Raina help me rediscover myself."

Katy enjoyed the drive home and even detoured to the mall to purchase some new jeans and a skirt on the way.

CHAPTER ELEVEN

STANDING STRONG

Garth called Katy twice Friday afternoon, but she didn't answer the phone. She went to the meeting in *her* car, as she still wanted to learn more about how to grow beyond her tragedy and the sessions really were helping her. She just didn't want Garth to feel obligated to help her any more than he had. He respected her unspoken request for distance and only greeted her cordially at the meeting and helped her with serving the snacks at coffee time.

The young mother, who Katy recognized from previous meetings, was sitting next to her during the session and struck up a conversation with Katy before the meeting resumed after the breaktime. She invited Katy to attend the Sunday morning worship services upstairs in the church, where she said she found great comfort in God's presence. She told Katy, the community of believers who attended that church were very supportive and not stuffy or religious, but genuine and caring. Katy felt a warm tugging in her heart and said she'd think about it, as the meeting resumed with a discussion on creating new holiday traditions, while honouring the memory of loved ones with commemorative ones.

Katy could feel Garth's glances, but wouldn't risk looking in his direction. She held her chin up and focused on the discussion. She would have to be strong from now on and get through this on her own. She could make it. She had to. She only nodded goodbye to him as she scooted out the door quickly, while the men were putting the chairs away.

The next week, Katy met again with Doctor Raina and together they went over the form she had completed. Doctor Raina, removed her glasses each time she spoke, looking Katy directly in the eye with compassion; and speaking with conviction on every point as together they worked through each item. Katy began to realize that a lot of her views on Rolf were based on her comparing him to the gentleness of her father and brother. She noticed that his family had been very militaristic and intellectuals, not given to displays of affection or "play". Everything in his upbringing had been practical, rooted in survival and based on his parents' experiences living in World War II Germany.

She began to realize that a lot of their differences were not only gender based, but culturally oriented as well. She began to modify the self-talk in her head that had judged him so harshly and began to better understand a lot of his behaviour and expressions. Doctor Raina then led Katy through a visualization exercise, designed to help her forgive Rolf and to forgive herself. It was going to be a long road, but she had started the journey, and as Doctor Raina had encouraged her, that was the most important thing.

Leaving the session, Katy wished she could have known earlier, what was becoming so clear now, and that she could have discussed it with Rolf… Of course, that was impossible, but, just like with Damien, she thought that she could begin to talk to him figuratively. Tell him how she felt, or what she was learning about their differences, and how she forgave him.

That night, Katy fell into a deep sleep. The tiger was again visible. Katy had a lion tamer's whip and chair in her hands. She fought valiantly and finally the tiger sat down in broken submission. Katy put down the implements and reached into the pocket of a safari jacket she was wearing. She took a key out and found it opened the "last door" which appeared behind her. As she opened the door, she saw Damien just on the other side of it. Rolf was there too, in the distance. He seemed composed and happy to see her. There was relief on both their faces and after a moment Katy shut the door, and put the key back in her pocket, patting it for safekeeping. The tiger began to follow submissively behind her after that, almost in a subservient capacity, or perhaps as a watchdog. Katy was no longer afraid of it and even turned to pet it once in a while.

Katy awoke feeling refreshed though she did not recall the dream.

CHAPTER TWELVE

HOMECOMING

On Sunday morning, Katy awoke a few minutes before seven and was feeling at peace. She decided getting her heart right with God might not be a bad idea, along with all that she had learned and done of late. She dressed in a conservative, designer, navy suit with a white silk blouse and wore her mother's pearls. She arrived just as the worship band began playing and sat near the back of the church. She was surprised to see that Garth was playing a bass guitar on stage. She was grateful that he hadn't noticed her arrival.

The minister spoke about how Jesus revealed the heavenly Father to us and showed us the heart of God. That He wants to have a personal relationship with each of His children and that He is working in each of our lives to draw us closer to Him.

At the minister's invitation, Katy bowed her head in a prayer of acknowledgement and surrendered to Jesus' Lordship and asked Him into her heart. She asked Him to take full control of her life and to save her from her sins. She spent the next few minutes of silence, giving him all her burdens and felt an *actual* physical sense of relief and lightness when the band began to play softly. She hadn't noticed the tears of joy streaming down her cheeks until an usher offered her a tissue. When she looked up, Garth was walking towards her and beaming. He enveloped her in his arms and whispered he was so proud of her. She nodded and sniffled, as he sat next to her for the meeting's closing prayer.

CHAPTER THIRTEEN

REVELATION

Continuing with the support group and weekly meetings with Dr. Raina were removing layers of guilt, pain and misunderstanding in Katy's heart. She was learning how our thoughts affect our words and our actions. She began reciting Biblical affirmations and seeing real change within herself. These were reflecting on the outside too. She looked and felt better every day and began taking an interest in her home again. By Christmas, she was feeling whole and secure in God's love. She enjoyed attending St. Andrew's Church and had made several friends there. She especially enjoyed helping out in the nursery once a month.

Katy helped Garth redecorate his house and took great pleasure in assisting him with painting it, and selecting art pieces to stage it for listing in January. They had made plans to have several of those who would otherwise be alone over the holidays to be at his house for Christmas dinner, and Katy was working on a special cat bed for Duffy.

One night, driving home from Garth's, Katy spontaneously found herself praying out loud: "Thank you, Lord, for my friend Garth. Thank you for all the positive changes You have brought into my life. I am amazed at all of the wonderful truth you have opened up to me and all of the precious people who have shown Your loving-kindness to me. Please continue to lead me deeper into a relationship with You and show me the path you have for the rest of my life. Let me know if I should take up the design business again, or if you have others plans for me. Amen."

She hummed a contemporary hymn and wondered what she should get Garth for Christmas. Then she began daydreaming about him and chided herself for letting her thoughts go beyond thinking of him as a friend. "Whoa, girl! You need to be careful, how you think of him. He's given you no reason for you to think of him, other than as a friend. "Lord," she said, adding a PS to her prayer, "and help me to keep my heart right, where Garth is concerned."

Katy resolved to keep Garth at arms length, and to focus on her relationship with God and friends. After all, he would be leaving soon, and that would be the end of it. He had helped her immensely, and now it was time for both of them to move on.

CHAPTER FOURTEEN

RESOLUTION

"Katy can I come over?" Garth's voice implored, as Katy answered the phone the next afternoon.

"Garth... I'm sorry, maybe it's not a good idea. I can't. I..."

"Katy, I found out something. Something important. I need to talk to you. Please. It won't take long," and he hung up.

Katy put the phone back on its base and wondered what the 'something' was, both hoping and fearing it might be about *them*.

Garth rang the doorbell and Katy let him in, then headed toward the living room trying to read his mood. Garth followed her. When she turned around, the graveness in his face arrested her, and she froze on the spot.

He began slowly, "Katy, I have a friend that I play squash with, James. He works at the coroner's office. He was away for a few months on a special assignment, but he's back in town, and I had him retrieve Rolf's file, just to see if there was any other possible explanation for the accident."

She looked shocked, hurt and pleading at the same time. He stared straight into Katy's eyes, and stepped closer to her. "Before I tell you what he said, I need to ask you a few questions. "Did Rolf have any allergies?"

"Well... yes. He was allergic to a lot of things: grass, dust, pollen... I always thought it was more fuel for him to complain about my housekeeping. So I just ignored his complaints."

"Well, according to the toxicology report, Rolf had a low level of histamine in his system. Also, the scene photographs showed a small welt, not explained by the coroner, on the back of his neck. Katy, is it possible that Rolf was allergic to bee stings?"

"Yes... yes he was! He was stung once, by a yellow jacket when he was in college, and after that had to carry a bee kit. He kept it in his car. Wait! He wasn't driving *his* car that day. He had borrowed a friend's four-by-four. Do you really think..."

"It's possible. Maybe there are other explanations, but this one seems plausible, and I don't think you should continue to beat yourself up, especially in light of this. Rolf may have been aware that he'd been stung and was too far from his bee kit or the hospital and panicked. Or maybe he passed out."

Katy's mind was racing, trying to grasp the possibility, the ramifications. She sank slowly onto the love seat by the window. "Oh, my God..."

Then a fresh wave of guilt, frustration and confusion assaulted her. Hot tears sprang to her eyes, and Katy buried her face in her hands.

She'd forgotten that Garth was in the room, until his sitting beside her pulled her back to the present.

Her mind raced. *He's got it all figured out. Got me all figured out. I was wrong. I'm always wrong. Wrong about everything. Somehow, I always knew it was my fault. It always is...*

"Oh, Garth. I was wrong. It's my fault," Katy cried out.

"Katy," he replied huskily, "It's not. It never was. Katy, don't you see? It's no one's fault."

He doesn't understand... doesn't care. I can't keep involving him. This doesn't concern him. Katy straightened her back, and wiped her eyes with her hands. "You're right. This makes sense. It is plausible", she sniffed. "Thank you for looking into it. You've done more than I could've asked. You've been a good friend and a great help. Thank you."

She went to stand up, but Garth, pulled her back down. "Don't you see? This changes everything for you. You didn't let Damien go with a crazed madman. It was an accident. A horrible, terrible accident. You have nothing to regret, or atone for. With your explanation about Rolf's allergies, the coroner will see the correlation, and amend his findings. You can finally be free, Katy; completely free from this nightmare. We can talk to him this afternoon if you want."

"We? No, you've done enough. You..."

"Shh..." Garth stopped her with his finger against her soft

pout.

"I'm here for the duration, not just this resolution. I did this for us."

"Us?" Katy asked in disbelief.

"Yeah. I knew you had to get this resolved before you could go on. And I'm not going on without you. We'll see it through together."

"You're a great friend, but you can't mean, you don't realize how..."

This time Garth prevented her spiel with his lips. His arms surrounded her with the warmth and security that she'd been aching for. He drew out of her the depths of longing she'd suppressed. The yearning and passion for life, for love, for... him!

There were no words. No more words. Only the rising, and falling of blissful heights and luxurious depths. Only the contented sound, of the tiger.

EPILOGUE

Reflecting on Katy's experience, we can see in life that it is easy to misunderstand. Especially when our lives are turned upside down by tragedy. Any traumatic event can cause a warped perspective. And the closer to home the event is, the greater the potential for distortion. It is almost impossible to discover the truth on our own. We need others, who are not rocked by the disaster, to relay information and provide feedback regarding our recovery and progress.

The human mind has a great capacity to heal and advance, if it is afforded a healthy atmosphere and time to regenerate; but one aspect of our nature is that we can be self-sabotaging, unless we have a friendly reminder to be patient and kind to ourselves, as well as to others who are "in process".

I've pondered the tiger in this story for a long time and have concluded that it represents our human soul. That is; the *capacity* we all have for fear, depression and immobilization: or for love, healing and action. All of these reside in this same human faculty. Whether it is dominated and broken; or overcomes and reigns in life, is determined by the choices we make. We have the freedom to chose *how* we will react to life experiences. This is our God-given privilege, the strength of the *tiger* in us.

Our *enemy* is never other people or circumstances, but how we view them, and the significance we assign to them is crucial to our wellbeing. God is our ally in this process and some of His greatest agents, are other human beings. I thank Him for the ones He has sent my way, to keep me alert to this fact. I thank Him, that He is always working in and around us, to bring us along, as we let Him.

But the God of all grace, who hath called us unto his eternal glory by Christ Jesus, after that ye have suffered a while, make you perfect, stablish, strengthen, and settle you.
   I Peter 5:10

CANICA ALLIANCE

For Laura, whose wonder and lovingkindness are pure inspiration. I love you so much, daughter of my heart.

CANICA ALLIANCE

A SEED IS SOWN - 2036

Juliana shut the Bible and smoothed her hands over its worn, black cover. It had been a dear companion for almost forty years.

"Father," she prayed, "may this, Your word, find another soul to nourish under Your guidance." She placed it in its sheath and sealed it securely.

She had no desire to resist the inevitable, and later that afternoon, reported to the euthanasia clinic as ordered, unaided, her mind on things above...

GLOSSARY OF TERMS

BUN: Bilinear Urban Navigator

Canica: An alliance of the United States and Canada formed in the year 2030

Knoll: Sensurround Personal Lounger

Nifto: Cool, hip

POD: Personal/Office/Dwelling

PAM: Personal Alarm Monitor

Sango: Hyper Nutrient Beverage
Be-stro: Be strong
Tube: Virtual Marketplace
MEM: Magnetic Encoded Mind
printer)

CONTENTS

PROLOGUE

This story takes place in 2055: a post-Christian era. The United States and Canada have formed an alliance, Canica, in order to compete in a global economy. World War III, which lasted only seven weeks toward the end of 2029, reduced the planet's population by half, having been precipitated by extremist ideologies. In the aftermath, it didn't take long for the United Nations to formulate and issue edicts that speedily decimated all traces of religious influences internationally.

Society is now run by humanistic systems designed to keep all life functions in check, and under the auspices of internationally uniform policies. Strict consequences are in place to quell any deviation from the status quo. Most of society, having conformed in the interest of peace and fiscal imperatives, is focused on producing a utopian existence, if only superficially.

All religion, having been identified as the source of conflict and war for centuries, has been classified with mythology and legends of the past, and deemed inappropriate.

In this sterile, controlling environment, a young Canadian woman sets out on her own to find truth and begins her own relationship with God… which changes everything,

CHAPTER ONE

2055 THE UNDERTAKING

Fifteen-year-old Cana sought solace in her knoll, but the synthesizer couldn't find an aura that suited her. Curling up in the padded, cocoon-lounger, she cried within herself, railing at the conflicting thoughts and feelings assaulting her brain. Thoughts of her tutorials, her friends' opinions, and her own beliefs spun, collided and sifted through her mind in a tumbling cacophony...

There is no God. The universe is governed by a "force," but whether or not it is intelligent, personal... Science has proven... Religion... society must adhere to established norms of behaviour for the sake of the whole...

What's wrong with me? Why am I so different from everyone else? she wondered. I try to be good... to go along with everything. Why can't I just accept what I'm told?

How do I know what's right? How can I be sure I'm right in what I think?

She stood and looked at her reflection in the window-mirror on the other side of her room. "Who are you, Cana Layelle Shiloh?" she challenged herself out loud, closing the distance and going nose to nose with her own reflection. "Who do you think you are?" Her thoughts continued, *Why do I have to question everything? I'm so tired of bucking the status quo... Defending my views...*

Cana groaned and threw herself on her daybed in exasperation, giving vent to the tears pressing for release. When it was over, she murmured brokenly: "I've got to get some answers, but how?"

Cana let her mind drift, not wanting to struggle anymore for the moment.

Once again thoughts of Juliana, the grandmother she never knew, nudged forward in her mind: *What was she like? What did she think of life? Of the world? Why was she... terminated?* Just then she remembered that her grandmother's Bible was stored, along with other mementos, somewhere in her cubby. When she was ten, her guardian Melanie, had given her the old, worn book sealed in a sheath and told her that Juliana had wanted her to have it. Back then, she just thought it was nifto to have a real book, and such an old one. She had never even cracked the seal on it.

Half-heartedly, she went to her air locker and sought it out. She stared at the strange book for several minutes, willing it to speak for itself. Part of her wrestled that it was only a mythological compendium, but another part, the one that often wondered about her grandmother, felt that it held some significance for her. And though she wasn't looking to it, or to her dead grandmother for guidance, she *was* looking for answers that would help her determine for herself, what life's purpose was.

It could be a jumping off place to begin her research, she reasoned. She turned it over in her hands, puzzling over what relevance it might hold for her. She held it in its acid-free casing, and reconstructed a familiar daydream about her grandmother, recalling old photographs and family movies she'd seen.

Emerging from her reverie, Cana considered what she knew about the book in her hands. She had learned about its general contents from her guardian and of course from her tutorials. It had been programmed into her humanities course, and thus into her by mind-print, that the Bible was a "pre-enlightenment speculation on the cosmos"... while treasured for its literary value, it was vastly debunked scientifically by the beginning of the twenty-first century.

Maybe this Bible holds secrets that would help me understand what happened to Juliana... maybe even Melanie, Cana mused, pondering her guardian. Impulsively, she broke the seal of the clear sheath and unwrapped the Bible from its covering.

"God," she prayed without realizing that's what she was doing, "if You are real, please help me find out the truth for myself".

Cana had a vague sense that this was the humble inauguration of a significant undertaking... her very own personal quest. She wouldn't even tell Melanie.

She must find out on her own what is truth, and though she felt unequal to the task, she knew that she was the only one who could undertake it. For by its very nature, it had to be a personal quest if the results were to be meaningful to her. She was prepared to make her own determinations and stand by them.

The fact that others didn't seem interested in knowing what life was all about, perplexed her. Most of her friends never seemed to question anything. All she knew was, that she had to know! This hunger had been growing in her for a long time, and today she would take an organized course of action: one that could determine her fate on an eternal scale. If there even was an eternity!

Her mind continued racing with thoughts that had been programmed into her since birth. She knew that what she was doing was questionable. Though it wasn't strictly forbidden, it was frowned upon to venture onto any informational avenue without a guide; but, because it was imperative that this conclude with personal convictions, she neglected to invoke her private trainer, an artificial intelligence that she called Sloan. Though she wondered if he really worked at all. Her grades didn't give him much credit. She always did much better on her own. Besides, she loved the satisfaction of discovering things for herself.

While gently turning through the fore-leaves of the musty book, Cana discovered handwritten entries that outlined Melanie's birth; as well as her 'Joining to Michael', or 'Marriage', as this Bible identified it. She also discovered that Melanie had a brother, Luke, who had been born three years after Melanie. There was no entry of his being married, or dead, or... anything. Melanie had never mentioned him. Cana wondered about this for only a moment and decided to forge on with her investigation. The only one who could tell her about Luke, was Melanie, and she wasn't ready to tell her about the Bible or her quest, at least not yet.

Throughout the pungent pages, there were highlighted passages and scrawled notes. Cana decided to start with these, since she didn't know where else to begin. Scanning the different chapters, divided by title as well as chronological numbers, she began to notice that Juliana had colour coded certain verses. One

of the first passages her eyes lit on was in a section called *Numbers*.
Accented in blue, it read:

The LORD bless thee, and keep thee:
The LORD make his face to shine upon thee,
and be gracious unto thee:
The LORD lift up his countenance upon thee,
and give thee peace.

It reminded her of her Shakespearean lessons, though she knew this was a King James version of the Bible. Cana caressed the page and wondered about the mysterious woman who provided for Cana's knowledge of her and her beliefs, even before Cana was born. Her grandmother, who had cared enough to leave her a cherished keep-sake; the only real book she had ever owned.

This benediction seemed a fitting launch for her objective. Cana closed her eyes and pondered the course before her. She was being drawn to an unknown destination and she was responding from a deep yearning within. The concept of an all knowing, all seeing, all powerful creator, seemed plausible to her. The universe had to come from somewhere, something, *someone*, she felt. She was excited at the prospects.

After scanning the pages a while longer, Cana closed the Bible and smiled with sweet satisfaction. She had begun.

CHAPTER TWO

LEX

"Melanie?" Cana called her guardian from her cubicle, "I'm not going to engage my per-com today. I'm going to the Bellis Fair Mall."

As she entered the cluttered space strewn with clothes, disks and snack wrappers, Melanie queried her daughter (for that was what she was no matter what the Alliance's legal take on the situation was), "Are you going with Hydra?"

"No, Cana said, looking up from her pack, "she has four quadrants to complete by Thursday. I'm going alone."

"Well, take your PAM with you."

"I don't know why we still need to wear security monitors," Cana moaned, walking into the nook to get a drink. "There hasn't been an abduction in over two years! And besides, I feel like a baby. I'm fifteen for gosh sakes!" ~~my sake~~ peace of mind,

"Please, do it for ~~my sake~~," Melanie said, following her. "I'll have a better day if I know you're wearing it."

"Okay, but the time is coming when I'm going to throw that thing into the vaporizer."

"You're not... going to the depilatory, are you? Your hair is so... pretty." Melanie said wistfully, gazing at Cana's chestnut curls.

"No, although everyone seems to be opting for the smooth-headed look again this year. Even Hydra. Her Guardian took her to the mall for an injection last Saturday."

"Cana, you know the potential side affects..."

"Yeah, well I don't have high enough grades anyway. I'll never get a parenting licence. Besides I can always adopt an artificial-womb baby if I ever do qualify for one."

"Still, it's a big decision," Melanie said quietly, taking the last of the laundry from the dry-cleaning unit, and walking back into her daughter's cubicle to hang it on clips in Cana's air locker. "I'm keeping my hair for now anyway," Cana said with a flippant toss of her head. "It's not worth a needle, to be nifto yet."

"And it *is* your decision of course," Melanie said lighter than she felt. "But I know what you mean about needles. When I was your age, everyone was getting their bodies pierced and tattooed. I was a coward, too."

"I'm not a coward! I just want to be my own person, do things on my own, not because someone else is!" Cana re-joined Melanie in the small space, and helped her put away her laundry. She lifted her chin and set her jaw.

Melanie nodded her recognition of this fact, and let the subject drop. It was true: Cana was never influenced by anything but her own determination on a subject.

Both a blessing and a bane, Melanie sighed in acknowledgement.

An hour later, after eating a nutrient bar, and chugging half a litre of synthetic apple juice, Cana caught the BUN outside her POD and was at the American mall in 12 minutes. She was looking for a kiosk that had some unusual optics, maybe some obsolete ones that would have an earlier perspective on philosophy, or humanities subjects. She could have summoned a lot of data on her per-com, but wanted the anonymity afforded her at the mall.

She hadn't noticed the two boys watching her from the food court, and was surprised when the one approached her. She almost triggered her monitor when he said, "You're from Vancouver right?"

"Uh—huh." Cana said, nervously racking her brain, wondering where she'd seen him before.

"We met last year at the Alliance Commemorative Social, remember? You were with the Omega Dance Troupe."

"Oh, ye-sss. You were the... stage hand that ran the synthesizer," they said simultaneously.

They both laughed. Cana, more from nerves.

Lex was still smiling long after Cana had quit laughing.

Finally, gesturing to his hairless friend he said, "This is Phenex. We live in Seattle. We're just here scoping, y' know...," his voice trailed, as his mind was preoccupied with Cana.

"Hi," Phenex interrupted. "Why are you looking in Saget's? They're so obtuse."

"I wasn't really," Cana responded quickly. "Just sort of wandering around".

"Hey look Lex, there's Raybin! I told you he'd be here today," Phenex said, his attention diverted.

"You go on, I'll catch up with you later. I'll just scope with...?"

"Cana," she said, wondering how to get rid of this intruder.

"Cana." Lex exclaimed keeping his eyes on her the whole time. "I'm..."

"You're Lex."

"You remembered my name from last year?" Lex brightened.

"No, your friend just called you Lex."

"Oh." Lex said, blushing slightly. "So whadya lookin' for? I know this place like the back of my hand," he gestured, pointing around the mall.

"Well, I don't know. I'm kinda lookin' for old disks. You know, old... tutorials," Cana broached cautiously.

"Why?"

"I just thought it'd be interesting to scope out the past, you know, for fun! I haven't really assimilated much ancient philosophy or humanities," she said lightly.

"I know what you mean," Lex said, running his hand through his wavy, black hair that had been shaved and coloured decorously in spots. "Our course-load has been so heavy since the latest Alliance directive, that I don't spend much educational slot-time on anything else. It's almost like we're not to question modern thought, only absorb it. There's no time for reflection, or processing."

Cana was surprised at Lex's candor, but found it refreshing. He wasn't a rebel or a free-thinking radical, just someone who could still express his own opinion and not just in-grafted rhetoric... Not like Hydra. She was so *predictable*.

"So my dear, will you allow me to accompany you on your quest?" Lex bowed low, sweeping his arm and causing his ebony sport suit to stretch taut over his muscular torso.

She nodded nobly and said giggling to Lex: "So gallant, how can I refuse?"

To herself, she thought: *Impressive! Hmmm... Maybe he can be of some assistance.*

The two speculators meandered down the concourse oblivious to everyone, including Phenex and his friend talking in an alcove with a business man who had joined them.

"I can't believe we got all three of these lines for just two hundred units! I'm glad you helped me scope them," Cana gushed less than an hour later.

"What now, my dear?" Lex said with such debonair gestures that for a moment, Cana imagined that they both were much older and very sophisticated.

Laughing she said, "Lex, how old are you?"

"Sixteen. I'll be seventeen in September. How 'bout you?"

"Fifteen 'til January," groaned Cana rolling her sapphire eyes toward the skylights.

"Just seven months to go then," he teased.

"Yeah, but my guardians treat me like I'm ten, so even when I am sixteen, it won't make much difference."

"They aren't restraining you in any way, are they?"

"No, it's nothing like that, they're law abiding. It's just that Melanie worries so much, and she's so sweet. I hate to trouble her. Besides, I wouldn't want to lose them. Melanie and Michael are my birth parents. I wouldn't want 'angels' who were just legal guardians. I'd always wonder if they really cared for me at all."

"I have legally appointed guardians, Lex said, kicking the floor. "My birth parents were found inadequate and relocated to an amelioration institution when I was seven. I was told they'd come back when they were rehabilitated, but I never saw them again. I hardly remember them, but I still wonder what became of them."

"Oh, Lex" she breathed, touching his arm.

"It's okay," he stammered, shrugging his shoulders.

She could see by his misting green eyes that it wasn't, but decided it was unwise to press.

"Thank you so much for helping me," she brightened. "Let me buy you a sango in the food court."

"No, I should catch up with Phenex," he gestured, seeing his friend heading for the exit. "We're going to a dance tonight. You, uh, wouldn't want to come would you?" He hesitated while turning to leave.

"No, my guardians are expecting me for supper. I'd love to if I'd planned ahead. But, I'm not dressed for a dance..."

"You look fine, c'mon!"

"No, maybe another time..."

"Well, can I call you?"

"I guess so. I'm listed under the Sana POD, in Vancouver. Shiloh, Cana Shiloh."

"I'll call you tomorrow, okay?"

"Sure. Be-stro."

"You too, be-stro."

CHAPTER THREE

FINDING A WAY

The next day while Cana was getting dressed, Michael hollered from the POD portal, "Cana? Melanie and I are going to the Loop for a strata meeting. Help yourself to lunch. We'll be back by six for supper."

"Okay. Bye." she called back to him cheerfully.

Cana had been waiting for her guardians to go out, so she could download her new disks uninterrupted. She did not want to explain at this point what she was doing. She put a protective code into the directory before she down-loaded the 'contraband' and made it resemble a file that she would write a journal into. It would be overlooked in a cursory security scan. She was only curious, not subversive, and wanted to avoid unnecessary scrutiny and the resultant screening interviews. Besides it would reflect negatively on Melanie and Michael if her queries were to be uncovered in an investigation by an Alliance security team. She entered trivia for the first ten screens. Since it was to look like a diary anyway, she decided to include some facts about Lex:

Met a boy at the mall today. So gorgeous. So mature. A perfect gentleman. I felt special beside him. Interesting how one individual can set himself apart from his peers in such a short period of time. Not just by his looks, either! Though they were impressive: midnight-black hair, tall and muscular, and this by physical prowess and not just steroids or surgical alteration! He told me that he competes internationally in a variety of athletics, including spacit.1

He's got a great smile, confidence, and a humorous, playful manner, without being obnoxious. He's almost seventeen! He asked me to a dance. I told him I'd like to go another time. I can't imagine what I'd wear. All my clothes are ancient. I'll have to get Melanie to help me pick out something on the tube.

Suddenly her percom jolted her ribcage, and even though she had been anxiously awaiting the call, Cana waited a prudent amount of time before responding.

"Hello?"

"Hello pretty girl."

"Lex, how are you?" She downloaded his image onto her per-com screen.

"I'm fine. Just listening to some Radovv tunes. Did you scan your text yet?"

"No, I was just about to. I wanted to wait until my guardians were out. You know..."

"Yeah. It's kinda clandestine. Kinda, *bold.*"

"Yeah, well, I'm no rebel or anything, but I wanted to explore some different tracks."

"Hey, it's fine with me. I'm a pseudo-rebel."

"A what?"

"A rebel at heart. At least when it comes to my thinking. I'm not going to *do* anything though. Just ruminate my ideas."

"Aren't you afraid to speak so freely?"

"Not to you. You're just like me... only a little more timid. You are an independent thinker. It's not illegal, just discouraged. Mostly if it causes the "thinker" to take *illegal* action, which I am too smart to consider. You *are* a free spirit, Cana. I bet you ~~can't,~~ don't even accept all the rhetoric on WWIII. Your concentration would be impeded by your logic. Am I right?"

[1]*Spacit is a sport involving six players apiece on two opposing teams with trap-door goals, and a synthetic ball, all of which are luminescent. It is played in a darkened, anti-gravitational chamber, with magnetic walls. Players wear electro-magnetic controls to propel and navigate around the court while trying to control the ball and sink it in the opposing team's trap door.*

"Well, yes, but I wouldn't express myself as candidly as you. I am new at this game. I never really considered exploring what *I* thought about things before. I've mostly followed what I've been taught. And besides, I don't think it's *all* wrong anyway. I mean, what would the world be like without some control factors? Remember what we learned about pre-Alliance Canada and America, before they formed Canica? And other countries like Russia and the rest of Europe?"

"So, my little brainstormer, what else is in your pretty little head besides these magnanimous thoughts?" Lex probed. He said this, almost like a condescending adult would. Not even like a guardian, or a tutor, more like a professional administrator who had *no* children in his home, or had ever related to one... someone who had no idea how to talk to young people. And her pride was hurt. So she didn't answer.

"Cana? Cana, what's wrong?"

"I'm more than a 'pretty little head!' Why do you use such archaic expressions anyway?"

"Sorry, I didn't mean to offend you. I intended to flatter you without coming right out and saying that I think you're nice looking."

"Nice looking, nice looking! You think I'm only *nice* looking?"

"Sheesh, I can't win with you! You're beautiful, Cana. Heck, I remembered you since your recital last year. I think you're great. Please don't be offended, I meant no harm."

"Lex, you're hopeless. It's a good thing I'm so generous and forgiving, otherwise you'd be vaporized by now, or at least disconnected."

"Well, before you cut me off...have you decided about a dance sometime? Like say... next Tuesday? The Roxy is having a half-price night. None of my friends can go. They all have mandatory tutorials that they're behind in grade sixteen. I could meet you at your place, or at the Roxy. It's at the Ladner Station in Vancouver. Ever been there?"

"No, but I'll meet you there Tuesday. What time?"

"19:00 hours."

"I should go now. I want to download this stuff and decipher what I want to keep and what I want to jettison before my guardians are back."

"If you insist..."

"Goodbye Lex. Be-stro."

"Be-stro, pretty girl."

Pretty Girl. Cana couldn't help relishing this now-endearing term just a few moments, and then continued her assessment of Lex a little longer...

First she committed his image to her MEM, then entered:

Lex is deep. No boy. A man. I must try to be as adult as him. 'Pretty' will only get me so far...

Wonder if he's got another girl. He was with the boys. Maybe he's 'mixed'. Whatever he is, I'm charmed...

CHAPTER FOUR

SPECULATION

Cana let the words whisk by her on her optical viewer, without linking to enter them into her MEM. She was scanning for something significant, hoping she'd recognize it when she saw it.

Phasing out...
Open discussion by officials selected...
...friendly terms of consolidation...
...children's classes were especially sensitive...
...nuclear family, a myth...
Political impurity must be eliminated.
...artistic expression must remain uncensored and freely distributed internationally.
...church income tax exemptions discontinued. Most organizations collapsed...
Educating its citizens is the responsibility of the state.
...twenty first century will be a post-christian era.
...refreshed from antiquated thinking...
... antediluvian values of the Judaeo-Christian ethic...
...that these teaching methods were archaic and unenlightened.

Cana rubbed her eyes and yawned.

"My guardians will be home soon and I still don't know anything," she groaned.

But when she looked again at the screen, some interesting tidbits were flashing by:

...heritage.

...spiritual reality.

...personal revelation of the call of God in the individual's life. We must endeavour to maintain the unity of the faith...

...Jesus Christ, the same yesterday, today, and forever.

Cana paused the optic track and reflected on what she did know.

Jesus Christ was a philosopher of the fourth millennia. He was a noted teacher, credited with miracles that were subsequently debunked by critics claiming they were at best eastern scientific displays or at worst hoaxes.

His love ethic was unrealistic.

His life and martyrdom affected uneducated, unsophisticated people universally for centuries. Only when the general masses were enlightened by higher education was this craft eradicated. This philosophy enabled oppressed peoples to withstand fierce dictatorships and merciless cruelties with exceptional stamina.

"Religion is the opiate of the masses. It quells the passionate, yet ignorant beast within the heart of the misguided," she quoted out loud, recalling her tutorials.

On that note, and feeling saturated, Cana exited the track and sought the solace of her grandmother's Bible. Cana spoke to the book in her hands, "Even if this is a mythological work, it is an amazing one. The passages I've assimilated from my recent study, have returned to my thinking over and over to comfort and challenge me. Perhaps I too am 'simple' and in need of an opiate," Cana smiled and said this sarcastically, thrusting out her chin.

Then, curling up in her knoll, she gently opened the Bible and smoothed her hands over each page as she turned them. She knew her grandmother had often handled the same leaves, and felt closer to her for the shared experience.

All she really knew of her grandmother was that she had died shortly after Melanie and Michael were 'joined' in 2035. After the Canadian/American Alliance was formed; and after World War III.

She had gone to a clinic and had been de-metabolized...

whether voluntarily or involuntarily, Cana didn't know.

Melanie had only said that Juliana had struggled with the 'new philosophy' and technological advances. She had longed for the old ways.

Whenever Melanie spoke of her, it was with distant melancholy, as though she were trying to remember what she was *really* like, or perhaps why. Cana never probed, as she preferred Melanie buoyant and open (at least to the degree that she was). There was an unspoken code of detachment they observed. It was typical of most POD's and Cana didn't question it. She only mourned it instinctively.

Halfway flipping through the book, she abandoned her reverie and began to read a passage highlighted again in blue:

The Lord is my light...

she paused to consider the meaning

...and my salvation. Whom shall I fear? The Lord is the strength of my life of whom shall I be afraid? When the wicked, even mine enemies and my foes, came upon me to eat up my flesh they stumbled and fell...

Cana saw a faded reference beside the text, it read:

The entrance of thy word giveth light. Psalm 119:130

She began turning the pages to find out the context of this thought, but she heard Michael and Melanie's voices in the POD portal, and quickly terminated her Bible exploration. She hid the book in her knoll, and activated a reclusive beach scenario, with a quiet, syncopated tune. She pondered what she had just read: that and her heritage.

For the first time, she felt a kinship with her ancestors, and wondered about their views of life, the world, the pre-Alliance world. She wondered about her mother's 'brother', Luke. At least she knew what had happened to her grandmother. She also knew her grandfather had died when Melanie was a child, but where, and how, and *who* was 'Luke'?

And how could she ask Melanie without upsetting her; without revealing her quest?

"Cana, did you eat? We're sitting down for supper if you care to join us," Michael called brightly from the eatery.

"Coming," Cana responded, realizing for the first time in a long time how warm and caring Michael was.

Over their kelp and tomato pizza, Michael and Melanie began discussing their upcoming vacation plans. Cana was lost in her own thoughts.

"Would you like to bring a friend this year?" Michael asked Cana. "Maybe Hydra, or Boyle would be free to check out Greece with us. Swimming is still permitted on the beaches there. Or maybe you'd like to test the salt water equipment I purchased on my business trip there last year? You could go exploring in the sea caves, or..."

Cana who had just clued in interrupted, "I — don't know yet. When do I have to commit?"

"We still have three more days before finalizing our arrangements with the travel bureau. Did you have other plans? You don't want to stay at the care facility while we're gone...?"

"No, no... it's just that Hydra is getting to be so boring, so, childish."

Her guardians looked at one another, and Melanie spoke, "Are you outgrowing her? Perhaps some new friends would alleviate your boredom. Have you looked in the directory? There's a new social club at the Library. They discuss inter-galactic phenomena and free ions... Everything from soup to nuts."

"They're nuts! I can't relate, Melanie. Besides, I did make a new friend... last week, at the mall. I'm meeting him on Tuesday at the Roxy." She purposefully neglected to tell them Lex's name, or his philosophical orientation. She wanted to check him out more herself first.

"Well, let us know what you decide," Melanie said quietly. She had learned long ago to suppress any controversial opinions she held, and this time was no exception. Michael furrowed his brow and went on eating.

After supper, Michael and Melanie retired early, and although Cana went to bed too, she was unable to sleep for a long time. Her mind raced with thoughts of her quest. She couldn't land on any solid conclusions, and didn't even try. She just mulled her new found ideas over, trying them on for size.

This caused more questions to emerge: *Is God real? What's He like? What does He want from me? Why did He make the world? Why hasn't He made His purpose clear to us, to me?*

When she finally drifted off, her dreams we're surreal and confused. Toward morning she finally settled into a cozy slumber and had a sweet dream of Lex. He was giving her a bouquet of botanical flowers that he had developed himself. He...

BRRRRRRRRRAPPP!!!

Her percom jolted her awake and she quickly silenced it with a groan.

CHAPTER FIVE

DETERMINATION

Despite her lack of sleep, Cana decided that this would be a beautiful day. The sky was as cloud-free as her mind. She was through her brooding, and was fixated on her tryst with Lex, and spent most of the day preparing to look her optimal best. She arrived at Ladner Station at precisely 19:00. Her cheeks were glowing and she moistened her smiling lips as she entered the building.

The Roxy was a large community forum often used for dances and sporting events, though Cana had never been before. *Hydra was too singular in her pursuit*, she reflected. *The mall was almost her exclusive destination of choice. It had everything she wanted. She'd said so herself.*

Cana stared in wonder at the spectacular scene before her. There were more youth there than she'd ever seen in one place before. They were all shapes and sizes, and attired in everything from Prehistoric to Space Odyssey styles. Most of the heads were bald and tattooed, though some were sumptuously tressed and she concluded they were probably wearing wigs: *No one has time for that much primping*, she smiled.

Bodies were cavorting in every imaginable contortion: sometimes alone, sometimes two or three in a tangle.

The music was loud and without lyrics, though some of the kids were mouthing the lyrics that Cana recognized sometimes accompanied the same tune when it was playing on her synthesizer: "I need to feel your need to feel me...," her mind recalled.

Once inside the quieter seating area, Cana saw Lex by the beverage bar and snuck up behind him.

"I know what you're thinking," she whispered teasingly. He spun around warily on his stool.

Recognition slowly dawned on his face. A large grin displaced his frown and he blurted out, "You minx!"

They both laughed, and he took her hands in his, admiring her from head to toe.

"How do *you* know what I was thinking? I might not've been thinking about you!" He teased back.

"Oh," she pouted, "and I even got a new outfit!" Then rallying, "Do you like it,? she said spinning around. "I blew my whole credit allowance."

Lex lingered over her turquoise-skirted unitard, as if trying to affix it in his memory.

"Yeah..., it's, it's great," he said slowly, looking past her.

"Lex, you're preoccupied, what's wrong?"

"C'mon, let's dance," He said ignoring her question and pulling her onto the dance floor. An instrumental ballad was playing. The low sweet music worked its magic on Cana and she imagined that she and Lex were alone in her knoll.

They were holding hands and moving freely without any design. There were several groups of kids around them, but Cana was oblivious. Lex led her away from the crowd into a quieter corner that replicated a twentieth century forest.

She grew concerned, when suddenly he turned around and she saw a serious look on his face.

"Cana, something's happened. My friend, Phenex, the one you met at the mall the other night, he's been apprehended. An executive with the Alliance baited him, to keep him for a 'love-toy'. Phenex is hooked. He loves the perks and is brainwashed into staying. He tried to talk me into meeting this executive's associate. Says he's looking for a new 'toy' too. Phenex told him I'd cooperate, but I skipped out."

"Oh, Lex. Are you alright? Where are your guardians? What did they say?"

"I didn't tell them. What can they do? They are **very good** party associates." This he said, as if he were recalling a distasteful experience.

"They are loyal to the Alliance and only see as far as the end of their own welfare. I'm expendable."

"Are you sure?"

"Pretty sure. Anyway, I wasn't about to risk their involvement. They have never done anything for me that didn't suit them. I doubt this would change their policy!" He said it so sardonically that Cana was convinced.

"What are you going to do?" She said, stepping even closer to him.

"I'm not sure yet. I've been thinking, but I don't want to act irrationally. My guardians think I'm at a new friend, Cain's POD. It will buy me some time. I wanted to see you. To explain to you, if I disappear, why, I..."

"Oh, Lex. This is terrible! I really like you. I don't want you to go away. What can we do?" Cana looked really worried now.

"Well, I always thought it was best to be prepared for something like this. Mind you, I thought it would involve something less distasteful... But I have made some contacts on the NET, and will have to see how quickly and secretly I can make arrangements."

Cana ventured, "My guardians are leaving next week on vacation. They want me to go along, but the thought of leaving you... How will I ever find you again?"

The trauma of losing Lex forged a stronger bond to him than Cana would have felt normally. She was behaving uncharacteristically weak, and began to fear that he would deem her an impediment, so she quickly whipped her emotions into shape, and calmed her voice. "I'm sorry, you've got bigger concerns than us".

"No, Cana. I care a lot about you," he said, as he closed the final distance between them. "That's why I came tonight. I, I don't really have anyone else. The guys you saw last week are my best friends, and yet, I'm not really close to any of them. None of them can help me, or probably even understand."

The tune changed to a louder, more raucous one. And Lex grabbed Cana's hand and spun her around." Let's forget about it for a little while," he shouted over the music. "Let's enjoy this time we have together."

He leaned in to her ear and spoke so only she could hear. "I'll think of something, don't worry. Don't worry your 'pretty little head'." He squeezed her hand and smiled in such a carefree, jubilant way that it gave Cana confidence that he would indeed think of something. With a silent prayer for his success, she let herself go along with Lex's shift in mood.

When they parted at the BUN station later that evening, Lex slid his arm from around her waist and placed both hands on her shoulders. She could feel his strength as his hands held her as firmly as his gaze.

"Cana, please don't worry about me. I will be alright. I'll contact you when I feel it's safe. This whole thing may blow over, but I just can't wait around to be apprehended. Thanks for coming tonight. It means a lot. I'll be thinking of you, always."

And with that he gave her a firm lingering kiss, and ran off to catch his train before she could think of anything to say.

Cana watched him until he was gone from sight, then turned and walked slowly toward the BUN. She decided to relish the evening. What they had, instead of the forces arrayed to wrench it from them. She hugged herself and smiled in reverie as she rode the train home.

How can I feel so close to someone I hardly know? It's like fate or something. I've never felt so trusting or close to anyone.

On the way home, Cana became determined to think of a way to help Lex. Her musings almost made her miss her station, but subconsciously her brain nudged her sufficiently to recognize her neighbourhood just as her POD was slipping by. She jammed the computer stop so hard that it flashed long after she disembarked.

Cana slept fitfully that night, and in the morning, she decided to broach her ideas with her guardians. At least *some* of her ideas. Michael had already gone out for a jog around the strata track, but Melanie listened as Cana informed her that she'd like to take her new friend to Greece with them.

Melanie knew that legally, she couldn't interfere with her daughter's wishes, but she also felt that as her counsellor she could help Cana explore her reasons. She could see that this boy meant a lot to Cana despite their short acquaintance, and was mobilized to protect her daughter as best she could.

"Cana, what do you know about this boy? I mean what message could you unwittingly be giving him, by inviting him along?"

"It's not unwittingly! I want him to know how much I care!" Cana was barely resisting tears of frustration and terror. She had hoped Melanie would acquiesce without a challenge.

"What about his lessons, his guardians? What do they say?"

"Lex is way ahead in his quadrants. His angels are neutral. You were willing to take Hydra! This boy is a lot more interesting than her. I would enjoy our vacation, rather than endure it. Besides, he's got the units. Hydra is always broke!" Cana wasn't sure if Lex had the units or not, but figured that together they could raise them, if necessary.

"Okay," Melanie conceded. "We'll discuss it with Michael when he gets back."

Cana went to her knoll and tried to contact Lex on his Percom. It was down, and Cana figured he was trying to protect her identity as well as lay low. All she could do was wait for him to contact her.

"Whew it's blustery out there today! Just the right kind of weather for jogging," Michael said breathlessly as he reached a tumbler to the beverage dispenser. "So, what've you two been up to? Anything worthwhile?"

"Michael," Cana began, choosing her words carefully. "I'd like to take a friend on our vacation to Greece. But, not Hydra. I met someone recently, a boy. He's smart and fun, and..."

Michael looked quizzically over to Melanie. She smiled wanly and shrugged.

"... and he's very athletic. You'd enjoy him too, Michael! I think we'd all have a great time!"

"Well, don't you think it would be good if we at least *met* this boy?"

"Lex. His name is Lex. Yeah, sure. I'll have him over. Then we can discuss our plans."

Cana hoped Lex would go along with her scheme. It would buy him some time, and they would be together and she wouldn't have to worry about him the whole time she was gone. And besides, it *would* be fun!

Michael and Melanie hadn't seen their daughter this animated in a long time. They were both intrigued and concerned. There wasn't much they could do if Cana decided to take this boy along, or opted to stay at a care facility for that matter. She was going to have to chart her own course. Though after she was asleep for the night, they would commit her 'charting' to the heavenly Charter.

Michael and Melanie were manifest pacifists, but covert rebels, both on their knees and with their involvement in the underground believer's netscape. They were an integral part of a system that afforded some latitude beyond the Alliance Directive. Though they only deviated for a critical cause, and under Divine direction.

Cana spent the afternoon in her knoll, willing Lex to contact her, and scanning her grandmother's Bible.

'*Divine Encounter,*' Juliana had jotted in the margin. The scripture beside it read:

There will I meet with thee, and I will commune with thee from above the mercy seat, from between the two cherubim which are upon the ark of the testimony...

Hmmm... Meet with, who? God, meet with who? Meet with me? I wonder..., Cana mused, considering the ramifications.

Then she gently turned and came upon a section called 'Joshua' and saw a passage underlined:

Have not I commanded thee? Be strong and of a good courage; be not afraid, neither be thou dismayed: for the LORD thy God is with thee whithersoever thou goest.

Cana felt that this was somehow a personal note of encouragement just for her. She resolved to commit it to memory.

Jarred from her reverie by her percom pulsating, Cana greeted Lex instantaneously.

"Lex?"

"Cana!"

"Lex, are you okay? I've been so worried!"

"Yeah, for now. Listen, I haven't much time. I'm trying to arrange for a passport. I'll be heading for Europe in the morning. I just wanted to let you know, well, that I'll miss you. I'm sorry this happened just now..."

Cana could feel the tears rolling down her cheeks and felt more powerless than she ever had.

"Lex," she ventured timidly, "I had an idea."

"What? What is it?" The gentleness in his voice encouraged her to continue.

"My angels are planning to take me to Greece in a few days.

104

I told them I wanted you to come along. It would buy you some time. We could sort this out together. I would miss you terribly if you just... left."

"I don't know. I'd have to think about it. I don't want to involve you. Maybe I'm over-reacting... just being paranoid."

"Well, either way, you're taking off for a while. Wouldn't it be better to have a friend?" Cana asked.

"Let me think about it, and I'll get back to you. I've gotta keep moving."

"Well, they want to meet you anyway. See if you can make your way here. No one knows about me."

"Phenex saw you, but I don't think he even caught your name. I'll think about it. Be-stro pretty girl. I'll call."

"Soon?"

"Soon."

Cana quoted part of the scripture that she was just reading to encourage him.

Lex was silent.

"Be-stro," Cana breathed, and then was cut off.

CHAPTER SIX

AWAY

The next morning Lex was at their POD before Cana awoke. Michael greeted him and chatted lightly until Cana was dressed. They discussed sports from around the world and throughout history. Melanie was getting them all hot protein beverages from the wall dispenser, when Cana joined them.

Lex was so relaxed and cheerful that Cana, buoyed up by his demeanour, played along. They acted like two good friends planning a great vacation rather than a great escape. Michael liked Lex right away. Melanie was cool toward him, but by the time he left, she had to admit to herself that he seemed 'okay'. Silently she prayed that their trip would be uneventful... whatever that meant.

They discussed the tentative plans for their trip and Lex said he would let them know the next day if he'd be going along.

Later when they were alone outside and Cana was saying goodbye, Lex answered his percom.

""Lex?, Phenex screamed over the device, "I've been trying to get ahold of you. Look, man, you were right. You've gotta get away. They already went to your POD. They think you'll try to expose the business manager. I made you some fake clearance i.d. I found an officiator in the guy's suite, while I was looking for some insurance to cover myself. It may only work for a little while, but at least it'll buy you some time. I'll give you the chemicals to make your imprints with."

Lex's head spun with the confirmation of his suspicions. "That was dangerous of you. Thanks," he stammered. "How can I get them from you?"

"Listen," Phenex said quickly, "I have a plan..."

"Cana, we *are* going to Greece together." Lex said shakily after he concluded with Phenex.

The charter was to leave four days later at 06:00 and Lex showed up at the Sana POD at 04:45, wearing his backpack and percom and carrying no other luggage.

"Good soldiers travel light," Michael laughed, as he motioned toward Melanie and Cana's six packed cases. Lex laughed too, hoping he didn't sound as nervous as he felt. When Cana entered the nook, he brightened, and gave her a hug. Melanie bristled, but said nothing. They all drank a quick sango and were on the BUN by 05:00.

They would be in a Grecian restaurant for lunch. Cana held Lex's hand the entire trip, even through the inspection station at Athens. Drawing on each other for courage they looked for all the world like two lovestruck puppies up to nothing more sinister than fun in the sun, Mediterranean style.

The brilliant azure sky and the aqua coloured water combined to make a wonderful tonic for Lex and Cana. They enjoyed water-skiing and underwater exploring with Michael and Melanie. They took long walks on the beach and talked of a million things, both silly and serious. By the end of the first week, they were no further ahead in solving Lex's problem, but they were secure in each other's feelings and confident that before they left Greece they would have a solution. Sure their love would find a way.

"Come on," Cana yelled over her shoulder. "You'll never catch up."

Her giant tortoise was five meters ahead of Lex's and showed no sign of letting up. Lex's had stopped to admire the tourists gathered to cheer the event and wouldn't be coaxed or hurried. Everyone was laughing, and Lex could barely stay on his mount. Only his competitive spirit kept him trying.

"Cana, watch where you're going," Michael yelled as her tortoise veered toward the edge of the boardwalk. She looked forward in time to see her dilemma, but not soon enough to do anything about it. Splash! she went into the drink. The crowd was really laughing now. Lex, hesitated only a moment before forfeiting his chance at winning altogether. The red-head from Spain would get the prize after all. Lex jumped into the water as a pretence of rescuing Cana. Her tortoise, Petunia was already climbing out the embankment, and Cana would have been out too, if she could compose herself, but she was doubled over laughing.

Lex offered her his hand chuckling, and he pulled her toward the embankment. At the last minute he ducked under the boardwalk and pulled her close, stealing a kiss. She pushed him into the water and ran out with Lex in close pursuit. They were breathless by the time they reached a grinning Michael, and Melanie who was snapping digitals of their reverie.

"Boy, you're fast," Lex exclaimed.

"Yeah, and my tortoise would've beat yours too, if she weren't directionally challenged!" Cana boasted giggling.

"Okay, you two, we have one hour till the sponge diving cruise. How do you want to spend it?" Melanie interjected practically.

"Do you want to go shopping?" Cana asked Lex, who hid behind Michael in mock disgust at the idea.

"Well, I was going to suggest a beverage." Michael offered.

"Sounds good to me." Melanie agreed.

Cana lowered her lashes and pouted ever so slightly.

"Okay, okay." Lex conceded. "Let's go, we've only got an hour."

Melanie chafed at having to let them go alone, but realized they'd already stated their preferences. She watched her daughter go off holding Lex's hand and silently willed them to do the right thing, now and always.

"Oh, look at the pottery," Cana squealed as they passed a booth in the open air market. There were clothiers and artisans hawking their wares as they had for centuries. Cana loved the natural sights and smells, the cornucopia of color and textures surrounding her. It was like walking through a history lesson, instead of just perusing a tutorial. She was pulling Lex down the concourse, when he stopped suddenly in front of a jewelry table.

With Cana watching, he picked up a small silver ring, engraved with symbols. He slipped it on her trembling right hand ring finger where it fit perfectly, and without a word to Cana, quickly paid for it and pulled her along beside him continuing their stroll down the midway, as if nothing had happened.

She exulted in the feeling of the ring on her finger and the knowledge of Lex's unspoken pledge of affection. She didn't want to spoil the moment with clumsy words either.

Later on the sponge diving boat, while watching the sunset, Cana thanked God for Lex's friendship, and prayed for their safety and guidance. Melanie, watching from the bow of the ship prayed the same thing.

CHAPTER SEVEN

REVELATIONS

A week later at the breakfast table, Michael announced, "Since today's our last day here, we've left it completely open for beachcombing, or lazing or whatever..."

"Lex and I are going down to the beach. He wants to try parasailing while he has an approved beach to do it at." Cana said.

Just then, Lex came out of his room yawning and stretching. That play was really interesting last night. Do you think that guy Jesus really existed, or is it just hype?" I mean, was he all they say he was?"

Michael broached cautiously, "Well, what do you think Lex?"

"I want to believe in God, in Jesus, but how can it be true? I mean, look at the world. Where is He now?"

"What if this is all part of His plan, Lex? If things are exactly as He intended them to be. Exactly as He foretold they would be?"

"Well, I think He'd have some explaining to do..."

"What if He already did that too?"

"Whaddya mean?"

"Well, how about if we talk about it tonight when you get back. I'll get some information ready for you and we'll go over it and you can make up your own mind about this Jesus?"

"Fair enough." Lex said and dove into his nutri-omelette. Later on that morning Cana and Lex found themselves with an international group of young people on a secluded part of the beach. A speed boat and all of the the equipment they needed for parasailing was waiting nearby.

"The wind is blowing from the northeast," the guide announced. It's a little stiff. Looks like a storm is brewing, but we'll monitor the conditions carefully. Should be okay for at least one pass.

Cana shivered, but one look at Lex's strong muscular build and the determination on his face banished her fears. She watched from the shore as the boat pulled her now dearest friend, out into the glistening waves. Lex looked back once and waved gallantly. Then soon, he was soaring above the water, looking like a prehistoric bird she recalled from one of her lessons.

She smiled to think of the sensations he was experiencing so free from the earth. Then, suddenly, horribly, he pitched awkwardly to one side, righted only partly and plunged again, mercilessly driven right into the water.

Cana screamed, like in a nightmare where it feels like nothing is coming out your mouth. Whether she had any voice or not, she couldn't tell. Several boats headed out from shore, and she ran to one nearby and urged the pilot to take her out.

They were pulling Lex's lifeless form from the water as she approached. Horror and tears clouded her sight as she threw herself around him in the recovery boat. Two men held her from crushing him, but let her gently cry beside him as others began CPR.

They finally recovered a heartbeat and shallow breathing, but Lex remained unconscious all the way to the clinic. Cana prayed her hardest during the transport and was unashamedly entreating a God that most of the people around her doubted existed. But she was oblivious to their stares. She was locked into a cataclysmic focus between Lex and her newly formed convictions. Everything she believed was on the line. Everything...

Melanie came into the waiting room first. She was quiet and pensive and wringing her hands while staring intently at Cana. Michael strode over and surrounded his daughter with all the love and strength he possessed, willing to take all of her pain into himself.

Finally a doctor came out of the examination room and informed them of Lex's injuries. He would be incapacitated for several weeks and it would be several days before they would know if his brain was damaged by the oxygen deprivation. He was in a coma, but he would survive.

"Ohhh," Cana expelled the breath she had been holding, and hugged Michael tightly.

"Can we see him?" Michael asked.

"Yes, but only for a moment, and then we'll need to ask you some questions," the doctor said.

"Oh, Lex! You're going to be alright. Everything's going to be alright," Cana said, tears streaming down her cheeks. She held his hand and stroked his temple gently. "Thank you, God," she whispered.

Melanie, who was on the other side of his bed holding his hand and silently praying, looked up at Cana, and then at Michael. Michael grinned broadly and winked at Melanie. They would talk later.

After a brief stay, the nursing staff shooed everyone from Lex's bedside.

"Now," said the doctor, "in order to submit my report, I will need some information. What is the patient's full name?" Melanie looked at Michael who shrugged. Surprisingly, they hadn't caught Lex's full name. They'd have to wait for Cana to come back with his pack from the hotel.

As Cana dumped the contents of Lex's pack on the bed back at the hotel, she noticed the fake i.d. prints.

"Phe-nex, Phenex Strall," she read incredulously. She knew Lex had done something to insure his safe exit from Canica, but assuming Phenex's identity...

How? What? The questions pounded into her brain, but no sense would come. She was running out of time and knew she would have to think on the way. She stuffed everything back into the pack and caught the BUN outside their hotel, determined to come up with a plan on the way to the medical centre.

Have not I commanded thee? Be strong and of a good courage; be not afraid, neither be thou dismayed: for the LORD thy God is with thee whithersoever thou goest.

The words ran over and over, floating up from Cana's heart, louder and louder until she found herself muttering them, drawing strength from them.

Then like a high diver on the precipice of the board, she knew what she must do. She must take a leap of faith, plunge into the great unknown and trust. Trust that this God, Creator of the universe, was big enough to meet her and Lex right here, right now.

"Excuse me," Cana said meekly, peeking into the doctor's station, can I have a word with Michael for a moment?"

"Sure, I was just going out for some sango," the doctor said. "We'll meet back here in fifteen minutes."

Michael rose to leave, then looking over his shoulder at Melanie's perplexed expression, gestured for her to keep calm, and was gone.

He ushered Cana to an empty lounge down the hall and sat facing her.

"Oh, Michael, it's awful, it's terrible. Lex is in danger. He's in trouble." Fresh tears began to flow, and Michael embraced his daughter with his arms and words of comfort. It's okay. He'll be okay. The doctor says..."

"No, you don't understand. He's, he's in trouble, he was in trouble before we ever came h-here." She stammered and shook so bad that Michael had trouble understanding her, but Cana quickly unravelled their tale of woe ending with her new found faith and hope that God would prove Himself able to rectify their situation, since it was beyond her to figure out how to.

"Oh, baby." Michael whispered into her ear. "My precious child. It's okay. It will be okay."

Cana sniffed and pulled back from him. "Did you hear what I said? Oh, what are we going to do?"

"Well, first of all," Michael said, We're going to get Melanie. Then we're going to have a family chat. Then we're going to straighten this whole mess out. I'll buy us some time with the doctor..."

Michael and Melanie shared with Cana their own faith in God and their fervent prayers since her birth, for her to come to a personal understanding of God on her own, since it was strictly forbidden to proselytize. That Melanie's mother's Bible had been so instrumental in her conversion, touched Melanie deeply and she told Cana what a godly woman her grandmother was and how pleased she would be to know of Cana's newfound faith.

They continued their discussion on the BUN and disembarked at a small POD on the outskirts of town. A handsome man with grey eyes like Melanie's answered the door. "Luke, this is Cana." Melanie said cheerfully.

"Hello, Cana," the man smiled offering his hand.

"Luke," Cana said weakly. "Your brother Luke?" Cana asked looking at Melanie.

"Yes, but how...? "

"In grandmother's Bible...," Cana said shaking his hand. "I am so glad to meet you. So glad that you are alive..."

Luke laughed, then hugged his niece. "Come in, I'm so glad to finally meet *you*!"

After they went inside, Michael explained their reason for being there and solicited Luke's help in getting Lex a new, safe identity.

"Luke is a hacker with the Christian Underground," he explained to Cana. "He doesn't exist officially, so he can do a lot of amazing things without any detection. He is one of the smartest technicians of the twenty-first century. God has gifted him to be able to function around the Alliance security directives. He has even devised a method of filling in cerebral crevices, neutralizing Alliance propaganda, a 'real brain washing'. What Luke does is extremely dangerous. You must never mention him to anyone, not even Lex, though I think Luke can help him out today without his even knowing it."

"How?" Cana wondered out loud.

"The Alliance isn't infallible, it's subject to human frailties, and human error. We just capitalize on its inefficiencies." Luke said, already busy at his elaborate, self-fabricated percom.

"Luke has developed a program to spot inconsistencies in the data banks and utilize them to our advantage." Melanie explained, putting her arm around her daughter. She realized that this had been a very challenging day for Cana.

"Of course, we rely completely on the Holy Spirit to guide and cover us. So far, we have functioned undetected. Near hits, have actually resulted in honing our skills, so that we are now buried several layers deeper than most technicians or security scans can access." Luke smiled as he said this. His confidence was comforting and inspirational.

Cana liked him... admired his courage and felt he really knew God personally. She was deeply touched when he told her that the ring Lex had given her was impressed with two of the most prominent Greek characters for God: Alpha and Omega.

They had to leave soon after they got there, but were assured that by the time they got to the clinic, the doctor would have already received Lex's new identity particulars.

CHAPTER EIGHT

A BRIGHT TOMORROW

Lex was in a coma for three weeks, though he always responded to Cana's touch by squeezing her hand, he did not come out of the maze he was in.

One day, his eyes opened and he looked around. When he saw Cana, his expression brightened. "Pretty girl!" he said hoarsely.

"Oh, Lex! You're all right. Hello!" She rose from her chair across the room from his bed, and ran to embrace him, almost tumbling on top of him. Then she kissed him quickly on the cheek and ran out into the hall to tell Melanie.

"Mom, come quick!" She whispered, motioning to her mother.

"Cana, where am I. What happened?" Lex asked weakly, when she came back into the private room.

"It's okay, everything's okay. You were in a parasailing accident. You've been in a coma..."

Two doctors had come in to examine Lex. They asked Melanie and Cana to wait outside.

"I'll be right back. I'll be right outside your room," Cana beamed.

When she came back in, Lex said, "Cana, I went away, or I had a dream. I saw Jesus; the man from the Bible. Cana, he is real. He told me he would send me back to you; to take care of you. To tell you he loves you. He is real, Cana!"

When Lex got out of the clinic, it didn't take him long to recover or to start asking questions too complicated for Cana, Michael or Melanie to answer. So once again they boarded the BUN to a little POD on the outskirts of town.

"Uncle Luke, I'd like you to meet my good friend Lex Blest."

"So, you're the magnificent Lex?" Luke smiled teasingly and watched Cana blush. "So good to meet you. Come in everyone. Come in!"

Lex was impressed with all Luke told him about God, His word, and about the work Luke was involved in. "I'd love to learn and to help out in anyway I can. I was a decent hacker on my own," he exclaimed.

Luke laughed and put his arm around Lex. "Sure, you're just what we're looking for! Someone with God, and no back door." Everyone laughed as Lex began to expound on some of his ideas for the future. Maybe he could even find his parents! He had a new perception and depth of faith, and Cana cherished him more than ever, especially now that they shared a spiritual dimension.

Cana let Lex revel in the moment and quietly slipped from the room. Once on the balcony she stared at the evening sky with fresh, appreciative eyes. "Thank you, God," she whispered, and bowed her head in acquiescence to all of His plans for her, whatever they may be.

Lex came up soundlessly behind her and whispered in her ear "Pretty girl, your parents and I have been working on a scheme that would make us neighbors. Are you game?"

"Oh, Lex," she spun around. Before she could say anything else, his lips found hers. Then his arms drew her very close. What could she say?

Endnote: 2 Thessalonians 2:

1 Now we request you, brethren, with regard to the coming of our Lord Jesus Christ and our gathering together to Him, 2 that you not be quickly shaken from your composure or be disturbed either by a spirit or a message or a letter as if from us, to the effect that the day of the Lord has come. 3 Let no one in any way deceive you, for it will not come unless the apostasy comes first, and the man of lawlessness is revealed, the son of destruction, 4 who opposes and exalts himself above every so-called god or object of worship, so that he takes his seat in the temple of God, displaying himself as being God. 5 Do you not remember that while I was still with you, I was telling you these things? 6 And you know what restrains him now, so that in his time he will be revealed. 7For the mystery of lawlessness is already at work; only he who now restrains will do so until he is taken out of the way…

ISLAND CHILD

For Angelika, whose spirit of adventure and stedfastness is boundless; and whose heart for God is strong and sure. You are the best of me, your father and your God. Loving you has been my greatest joy, my darling child.

CONTENTS

CHAPTER ONE

A DREAM LIVES

Reclining on a chaise lounger overlooking the point at sunset, Annette sighed contentedly as she wrapped her shawl a bit tighter around her shoulders. It was cooling down significantly in the September, evening air. Had it really only been four years since she and the children had returned to Prince Edward Island to pursue her late husband's dream... their dream? So much had happened. It seemed like a lifetime ago.

And yet in other ways, it seemed like only yesterday. For she could vividly remember their first few weeks. Back then she wondered if they would really be able to accomplish their goal. Would the money be enough? Had they done their homework?

She had been reluctant to continue alone on the path that she and David had planned together before he was killed in a car accident, and yet what else could be done? Everything had already been sold, packed and transported. It was the only logical step. How insurmountable it had seemed back then, to undertake such a huge endeavour without David. Without his calm, decisive, management abilities. Without his enthusiasm for the project. Without his loving. Without.......him.

She and the girls only had the house plans that the architect out west had drawn up, their savings, the insurance money and a few "hopeful" clients who had pledged online. "Out west..." the expression seemed foreign now, but before, when Vancouver was home, "out east" was the great unknown: only a delicious dream birthed while they were on vacation one summer in P.E.I. A dream that had taken on a life of it's own... a hope filled with promise of a brighter future for their family, in this beautiful place.

Part of what fuelled her after David's death, was the noble notion that it would make his legacy more meaningful if she followed through as a memorial with the plans that they had forged together. Otherwise, she never would have had the courage to venture into this daunting project on her own.

Annette recalled the realtor, Mr. Abbot who had shown her around the island. He knew from their email correspondence what they had been looking for in a property, so it didn't take long for them to find the perfect spot because of his pre-culling. It was as though Providence had carved the perfect niche long before Annette was even born. She felt such a sense of destiny when she first espied "Shiloh". Of course it wasn't called that then. In fact, it had no name at all. Most places on the island didn't. But Annette had felt a kinship with P.E.I. author, Lucy Maud Montgomery's "Anne of Green Gables" and was affectionately inclined to name her beloved homestead on Prince Edward Island, just as Anne had named all of her favourite haunts. She chose Shiloh, because it meant 'peace'.

Peace she cherished. Peace was good.

Back then, many of the construction trade workers were glad for the elaborate project that Annette's assisted living/bed and breakfast facility presented. It meant work that would last through the fall and maybe even into winter if the weather held... but they had worked so heartily, that they came in under budget and under time even finishing the landscaping the first week in November.

That first winter, her daughters, Bridgette and Alise, had rambled aimlessly around the large, sprawling structure, but by Spring, Annette had it furnished and decorated to suit her taste, staffed it, and the first tenants had begun arriving.

Already at fifteen, Bridgette was quite capable of running most of the household single-handedly. She was... efficient (so like David). Though the other staff managed their duties quite nicely, Bridgette had to have her finger in every pie. Though piloting the horse barn, was what "Bridges" enjoyed best of all. Which suited everyone else just fine. In all likelihood, there probably wouldn't even be any horses if it weren't for her. No, she was definitely the queen of the stables, to be sure.

Alise on the other hand was demure, gentle and domestic. At nine years old, she loved nothing better than to curl up in the sunroom with the latest Kidz™ magazine or paperback chapter book. She'd checked out just about every one shelved at the Charlottetown public library (some twice). And, she was especially good company for the elder folk. She was always cuddling with Grandma or baking and delivering wrapped goodies to Miss Martha. She could hold her own in checkers with Grampa too.

Annette doubted that Alise could remember life before Shiloh. She struggled to retain memories of her Daddy. Which is why they had made a memory book last year. It contained pictures and recollections of Alise's special times with her father. She and Annette read a page or two almost every night.

No, they had made out okay. The house had been full that summer. They even had a few bookings for next year already, such was their reputation now. Some families were looking forward to returning. Others had heard about the inn from their friends who had come home bragging about their wonderful vacation, and they wanted to make sure they secured the experience for themselves next year.

The last few guests had left on Tuesday, and the staff were looking forward to a well-deserved rest. Some were heading south for the winter, or at least part of it. Not that things were shutting down completely. There was a necessity for some to stay and maintain the place for the older folks; local "grandparents" who had moved in and the girls had adopted: Miss Martha, a retired school teacher, and Uncle Pete (a disabled, homeless man Annette had met while volunteering with the Salvation Army™ – who needed nothing but a loving home to set him aright), Grandma, Grandpa, Annette and the girls. And of course this was the time to regroup for next year. Preserves to put up, repairs to undertake, sprucing up and plans to make...

No, they would definitely need a skeleton crew through the winter. With some going and others returning, things would run along just fine until the first tourists arrived in the Spring.

Annette savoured the brisk breeze that was whipping around the point. The sun was just about completely set now and she could barely make out the shore at all, let alone Lennox Island just eighteen kilometres offshore from Malpeque Bay. She took a deep breath of the salty air. It was the end of a full, but satisfying season.

Annette lingered a few minutes more before stealing into the house and preparing for bed. "Thank you, God, for seeing us through to this juncture," she murmured once under the covers. "We never could've done it without You. Please continue to keep Your hand on us and give us the direction and the stamina we need to carry on the work You have given us to do. We trust You."

CHAPTER TWO

ROOTS AND WINGS

Finally, warmer days came, signaling winter was losing its grip and the quiet days began to give way to hectic ones.

The April Mi'Kmaq Native Festival was scheduled in two weeks and this was the first year that Annette felt she and the girls could get away for a long weekend at that time of year. She had relaxed to the point that she felt confident that Molly, the housekeeper and her husband James, who both lived on site, could run things for a few days without her input. James and the "kids" practicum students from the community college, and the youth outreach program's graduates, could manage the domestic duties and the grounds. There wasn't too much to do just yet... Maybe next week the garden could be turned over...

"Mom?" Have you seen my yellow sweater?" Bridgette called down from the second floor.

"It's in the laundry room," Annette answered her, and then turned back to Molly and their conversation.

Molly passed a basket of banana nut muffins to Annette and then poured more tea into her cup. Annette smiled at her confidante and covered her free hand with one of her own. "I was thinking about taking the girls to the Mi'Kmaq Festival next month," she said warmly. "You and James can manage for four days, eh?"

"Of course," Molly put the teapot down and covered Annette's hand with her other one, then patted it. "We'll be just fine."

Annette loved the lilt in her, now dear friend's maritime accent. She took a deep breath and grinned even bigger, exhaling. This was going to be a great getaway and a great Spring. She could just feel it.

When their departure day arrived, Annette gave Molly and James a few more last minute instructions. Even though everything was set out in the log book, she couldn't help herself. The older couple nodded reassuringly and smiled calmly. The twinkle in James eye, made Annette realize how silly she was being. For a moment, she thought of David, of his strength, and his faith. She gave them both one last hug and ducked into the Jeep™. Everything *would be* just fine.

CHAPTER THREE

MARITIME ADVENTURE

With a final wave, Annette and the girls drove off to enjoy the local colour and act like tourists themselves.

The Mi'Kmaq community was situated on Lennox Island, eighteen kilometres from of the main island and had a completely distinct atmosphere. Especially now with the annual cultural celebrations under way. Annette drove the Jeep off the ferry and surveyed the scene.

The community's central district was bedecked with art and regalia, with full participation from all of the tiny island's residents. The day was turning out to be perfect. The sun was burning off the morning mist; the ever present sea was pleasantly providing background ambience; and the rebirthing tokens of Spring were evident everywhere, harmonizing with a symphony of fragrance and colour and life. Fishing boats were polished and gleaming in the wharf, as the cannery and seagulls provided an ambient backdrop echoing the village's quaint heritage.

Annette was especially thrilled to see little shops lining both sides of the main dirt road. Though they were similar in appearance, each was unique in it's own way. There were eateries, leather and bead shops, wood craft stores as well as an open air market at the far end; all positioned strategically before a large open field – which had horses tethered along one side and fairground tents on the other. Annette recalled the website had referenced a rodeo and traditional dance exhibitions. She noticed Bridgette craning her neck to see if she recognized anyone she knew. Horses were such a part of her life now and Facebook™ connected her to the local equestrian world. Annette let her know they would make their way there eventually, but they had to stick together. Her oft-repeated safety talk soon followed, and both daughters finished her final sentence with her: "Always have a buddy, even if you're just going to the bathroom!"

Two art galleries were halfway up the block and visitors to the island were pouring from the street into them both. Annette could see why. Even from her position at the beginning of the block, she observed some impressive paintings and carvings in their windows. She was taken in by them too. An excitement was in the air. The mood of the crowd was amiable and community oriented. Annette had always loved natural environments with earthy artisans, having avoided commercial "plastic" destinations all her life.

Eventually, after indulging Bridgette with an ice-cream cone and Alise with a bannock beavertail, she led the girls to the closest gallery, situated behind makeshift display tables featured out front. Parade participants were just beginning to congregate in the field on the corner and the girls were oohing and ahing at their elaborate costumes. "I'll just be in here for a few minutes, don't go anywhere," Annette admonished, gesturing toward the store, as Bridgette and Alise waved her off, only half listening.

The girls stood outside watching traditionally blanketed band elders and native dancers beginning to arrange themselves, along with an array of other participants: band youngsters, horses, tom-tom drummers and mythological ancestral characters in readiment for their procession down the parade route. Folks began gathering on both sides of the street.

"Ohhhh," Annette breathed, as soon as she entered the sanctuary of the cooler gallery pungent with odors of natural materials; cedar, leather and lavender. She spied a spectacular painting of the big island, as viewed from the shores of Lennox Island. It was a morning view at sunrise. It was pristine, probably toward the western side, somewhere near her point, apparently created before her arrival she concluded, as there were no man-made structures visible in the scene.

Annette thought she recognized the location, but wasn't sure. When the curator came near, she inquired as to the location of the painting.

"Gillis Point, I think," said the woman. "Isn't that right, Shane?

He painted it," she explained to Annette, pointing to a man partially concealed behind a printed deer skin canvas. He was talking to another customer and so, as he finished, he queried,

"What's that Michelle?" He said this leaning backward and placing his six foot plus frame into full view.

"This is facing the north-west bluffs, isn't it? Towards the point past Malpeque Bay? Michelle restated.

"Yes", he smiled, nodding his head.

And what a smile. It was more like a flash of light, or lightning - and had a magnetic quality about it. Annette felt herself staring. She didn't know what it was about him, but this artist had an endearing quality that made her quiver. She turned back to the painting, partly to shield the blush she felt rising on her cheeks. It was something so foreign and unbidden that she was in semi-shock. Captivated by the painting (yet still haunted by it's creator), Annette studied it thoughtfully, while Shane slid quietly beside, yet slightly behind her.

"I *do* know that spot; exactly," she stated pleased with herself. "It's not far from our place." She said this absently, not meaning to mention anything of a personal nature. She turned to acknowledge Shane, and only then realized his proximity.

"Ah, one of my preferred locations on the coast, it's so picturesque, so... compelling." His words were enunciated with a distinct Maritime-Acadian accent overlaying an aboriginal tongue full of strength and calm. "I painted it five years ago. It's one of my favourites. Only recently have I felt able to part with it. Of course, now there's a large estate there."

"Yes, Shiloh, that's our place, mine and my daughters," Annette said softly while turning slightly again, to look up at him.

"Have you lived on the big island long? I've never seen you before," he beamed, obviously taking her in approvingly.

"For four years," Annette confessed looking down, feeling more like an outsider than she had in a couple of years and not sure how he viewed the development of natural landscapes.

"Oh, well, I only get over there a few of times every summer," Shane offered shrugging casually and letting her off the hook. "Otherwise, I'm sure we'd have met. I'm Shane Denoir and this is my sister, Michelle," he said gesturing to the woman, but did not remove his gaze from Annette. Michelle smiled in acknowledgement, nodding slightly.

"So, you like 'Le Bonne Soleil', eh?"

"Yes, very much. In fact, I'd like to buy it," Annette said, regaining her composure. "I'd like to hang it in our foyer... Er, we, uh, Shiloh is a Bed & Breakfast on the bluffs near Gillis Point. Though we also have a few permanent residents." Then she bumbled to explain the 'we'.

"I know the place" Shane acknowledged, as Michelle slipped away to attend to another customer who was eyeing a relief carving. "The old Doucette property. Yes, I've seen it, on route twelve just past the Provincial Park?"

"That's right. Well... if you'll wrap up this piece, I'll see if I can get it to my Jeep." Annette gestured toward the direction her vehicle was parked.

Almost too quickly, Shane offered: "I'll be round your way on Tuesday if you want, I can deliver it in my van and help you hang it. I'll be taking some other paintings to guests staying at the White Sands who are flying out that afternoon. I could come by after that, say around noon?"

His smile was dazzling and Annette couldn't form a word for a second. He stood and waited calmly, patiently, bronze toned and deep-eyed, exuding tranquility.

"O-okay," Annette stammered, willing her mind to unfreeze. "427 Rue de Chateguay... Shiloh, is the name of our inn."

Shane extended his arm graciously to one side of his muscular frame, escorting her to the till and just as she finished paying for the painting, a high school band outside started playing a light-hearted medley. Annette stuffed the receipt in her purse and said, "Thank you," excusing herself to rejoin her daughters, a sense of wonder wrapping itself around her.

Bridgette had finished her ice-cream and Alise was eager to join in with some children who were dancing on the side of the crowd nearest the approaching performers. The parade was an obvious community affair with good natured cheer all around as locals and visitors interacted jovially.

Annette took it all in with a grateful heart. Later, while the children explored the fairgrounds with new friends they had made, Annette joined a few of the local women in the cultural centre for tea and cookies. She learned a lot about the Mi'Kmaq people and their traditions, making a mental note to study more on the internet once she returned home. A well-educated, kindly woman named, Annie, lingered longer than the rest, and exchanged contact information with Annette.

Annette had arranged for she and the girls to stay in a bed and breakfast on Lennox Island, even though they could have easily gone home each night. She had wanted to get a good rest and the change of environment would facilitate that. She only answered two texts from Molly and by the end of the third day, was unwinding completely. As they hiked along the shore on the outskirts of the village, they walked past an old, but well-preserved simple Catholic church. They slipped inside and viewed the stained glassed windows and well-worn, burnished pews with padded kneeling benches. It smelled musty and the floorboards were worn, but it felt like a hallowed place. Candles in red glass holders flickered to one side and a simple crucifix was above the altar.

Annette wondered at the Christian influence on the island's historical residents and pondered with respect, the mystical feel of the edifice. She turned her heart toward God and communed with Him in the sweet ambiance of the cool quiet. She would have lingered longer, had the girls not urged her on. When she stepped again into the sunlight and breathed in the salty air outside, it was with fresh perspective and vigor. She was optimistic about the future and felt instinctively as if Shane, or perhaps the residents of Lennox Island might figure largely in that future. She smiled at the thought.

The girls' new friends and Annette making a business connection with the owners of the clean, tastefully decorated residence they stayed in, made the trip especially enjoyable, and everyone agreed to keep in touch. She couldn't believe how rejuvenated she felt and made a mental note to schedule more getaways in the future. Annette recognized how the late night talks and the shared experience had made her and her daughters that much closer, and that meant everything to her. Her thoughts went to David, as they often did and a fresh wave of nostalgia washed over her. She wished he could be there to see how well they were doing. Then, she thought, perhaps, in a way, he was.

She considered what he would think about Shane, and she knew, just as quickly, that he would be the first to approve. He would want her to be happy. Then she chided herself, because, who knew what Shane was thinking?

CHAPTER FOUR
CONNECTIONS

Tuesday morning was overcast and the ocean was choppy. Annette wondered if Shane would in fact venture over, or wait for a calmer day to transport his treasures. Of course he would come, the tourists from Scotland were departing today and he had their paintings as well. That thought cheered her and she bounced jauntily downstairs to breakfast.

"Hey, what's up, Mom?" asked Alise, who was sitting in the nook having a bagel and chatting with Molly. Annette toned down her smile a notch, tickled her daughter to distract her from the question, and looked intently out the kitchen window. She could see that James was already in the yard, tending the vegetable garden. She could also see the morning mist rising from the lawn. Then, looking further toward the horizon, she again noted, the sky was completely grey without a patch of blue anywhere. Just as her mood was slipping to glum, she remembered hearing the forecast called for "partly sunny" and decided to hope for the best.

"I just love Springtime," Annette exclaimed brightly, giving her daughter a tight squeeze and smiling at Molly, before pouring herself a cup of coffee and joining them.

"A delivery should be arriving today," she advised Molly nonchalantly, "a painting I purchased at the festival."

Once Bridgette and Alise left for school that morning, Annette poured over the books, double checking all her figures for the upcoming season, insuring she hadn't neglected anything. She made a few phone calls and found extra reasons to stay on the ground floor, so she didn't miss Shane's arrival. Normally, she would have spent the morning in her suite on the third floor, unpacking and sorting laundry. Instead, when she finished in the office, she visited with Grandma, Grandpa and Pete in the living room. Miss Martha was away visiting her niece in Maine. Annette loved that their household could care for senior citizens in addition to running a hospitality venue. The girls would grow up having the values that David and she had so wanted to instill in them; including caring for those more vulnerable.

Finally, she excused herself, having decided to wander through the foyer, into the sunroom off the kitchen at the back of the residence, to check once more on the weather over the water, when the doorbell rang. It naturally fell to her to answer it and she flushed only slightly before opening the large mahogany front door. After exchanging pleasantries, Shane and Annette settled into an amiable conversation about the weather, the weekend, the festival and Shiloh. They hung the painting, and when Molly announced lunch, it was no big thing for Annette to invite Shane to join them and for him to accept.

Shane was an effable guest, charming everyone with his light-hearted stories. It was obvious he was well educated and comfortable in his own skin. Each person around the table found at least one common interest with him and he surmised that Annette's heart was as big as the all outdoors, given the nature of her enterprise and the motley crew she'd assembled.

Neither Annette or Shane wanted their visit to end, but when afternoon tea extended toward suppertime, Shane excused himself under the guise of good manners, referencing his need to get home in time to close up the gallery... but not before inviting Annette to join him for an afternoon drive to see some unique places on PEI during his next scheduled visit a week away.

Later that night when the girls were asleep, Annette reflected prayerfully, on what she had learned about Shane. He had a job as a cultural arts professor at Toronto University. He had a passion for the Mi'kmaq people, his people. He lived in a suburb of Toronto, but spent his holidays and summers on the little island with his sister Michelle, running the art gallery; and assisting with the band's fishing business. He was taking a one year sabbatical in order to finish his doctoral thesis on intercultural relations and would return to teach in September. He had learned that she was a widow, following through with the dreams she and her late husband had agreed on before he'd died, and that she was a capable, effervescent gal, with a sweet sense of humour.

The next week, by the end of their drive around the island to Shane's favourite spots, Annette and Shane had built a bridge of understanding and care between them. He spent the rest of his Spring vacation with her. Michelle understood. She could make do with her usual staff at the gallery. It was in the summer, when the bulk of their business occurred. Shane would definitely be needed then.

Annette enjoyed the attention Shane gave her and since he was only in town for eight more days, she reasoned that the estate and the girls could manage without her 24/7 as well.

The time went quickly and it was harder than she thought it would be to say goodbye to him, but with Shane's assurance he would be back in seven weeks for summer vacation, she resolved to make the best of it. Those seven weeks were filled with phone calls, emails, texts and a few floral arrangements arriving at Shiloh for Annette.

CHAPTER FIVE

LOVE BLOSSOMS

Two days before Shane was due back, Annette had made all of the necessary arrangements to free up her summer as much as possible, in order to spend time with him, even if it meant her helping out at the gallery. Bridgette and Alise were to spend the summer with their paternal aunt and her family in Vancouver and Molly, James and the fresh interns were well-prepared for the onslaught of tourists. A couple of locals had been hired to augment the crew. Annette was confident in their abilities and elatedly looked forward to the summer.

She spent her last day alone at a local spa. Annette wanted to be fresh and relaxed when Shane arrived. She had a manicure, a pedicure and a massage. She picked up a new dress on her way out of town, and the next day, she arrived almost an hour early to pick Shane up at the Charlottetown airport.

Shane took Annette out to his favourite restaurant in Summerside, where they dined on fresh salads, lobster, baked potatoes, red wine and chocolate cake. They talked and laughed until their jaws hurt. They went for a sunset walk along the shore holding hands and talking some more. It was after midnight when Shane finally parted from Annette and took his family's skiff to his home on Lennox Island.

Summer was packed with work, outings, and making plans for the future. Shane proposed to Annette on July 1st, in Victoria Park on the Charlottetown waterfront, right before the fireworks celebration. She jumped into his arms and let him put the white gold ring with a solitaire diamond on her left hand. She was ecstatic.

He held her tight and closed his eyes, letting the jubilation get the better of him. By the time he left Annette, they had rough plans for a Thanksgiving wedding in October. She would make most of the arrangements and he would help her finish up when he came back on the Thursday before. Bridgette and Alise were overjoyed when their mother told them the news, but were both worried it might mean they would have to move away from their friends and school. Annette assured them that Shane would be moving into Shiloh and that he had taken a federal government job as an attache to the First Nations peoples in eastern Canada. He would be travelling a lot, but they would see him more often than they had before.

Everyone was happy with this arrangement and wedding plans dominated interests of the household.

CHAPTER SIX

DISCLOSURE

One dark, rainy night in mid-September, after he was home in his Toronto apartment, Shane read a letter sent to him from Annie on Lennox Island. Annie was the mother of his first love, Sherrie. He slowly took in the words she had written him. Words that shot right through him. Words that brought him low:

Dear Shane,
I know you will find it strange receiving a letter from me. I have something to tell you, that I feel will be best told in writing. I trust I have made a wise decision.

Before Sherrie drowned, she spent the earlier part of that year in Saskatchewan with my sister. Perhaps you recall that. What you, or no one else knows, is that Sherrie was pregnant. She never wanted you to know.

She was ashamed to admit to me, how she had come to be in that state, knowing my beliefs. But she told me how she had taken advantage of your inebriated state, the weekend before you left for the University in Toronto. How she had seduced you. She was desperately trying to get you to change your mind about going. So she threw herself at you, hoping madly to captivate you.

Later, she wondered if you even remembered. You never mentioned it, she said.

She regretted it immediately, and acknowledged your right to choose your own destiny, with or without her.

You weren't wrong to make the choices you did. Neither of you were ready to make a serious commitment. And Sherrie realized that more and more as time went on.

Unfortunately, she found herself with child, and decided it was best to give that child up for adoption.

We were able to conceal her pregnancy for the first six months with baggy clothing and smocks (they were in style then). Even her father didn't notice, and I never told him.

My sister's husband was a social worker and he made all of the arrangements. The baby went to a childless couple. The wife was part native, a nurse I think.

Sherrie came home after recovering for a few weeks, and made me promise to never mention the matter to a soul. A promise that I've honoured. Until now.

Shane, the child, your daughter, called me earlier this week. She had traced her birth records via the adoption registry in Ottawa. I told her about Sherrie. She asked me about you. I told her that I would be contacting you and informing you of our conversation.

I've been mulling the whole thing over for two days. Wondering how to tell you. Then this morning, she, her name is Willow, called me again. Willow would like to come visit over Christmas break. Whether you want to meet her or not, she wants to meet me, and learn more about her natural heritage. She says her adoptive parents are wonderful, and very supportive of her making this pilgrimage. She says she just has questions that she wants answered in order that she might have peace. I can understand that.

So, my dear Shane. I am sorry that you had to find out.

I never would have broken my vow to Sherrie, if Willow hadn't turned up asking me to. Perhaps it is for the best. I think Sherrie would understand.

If you want to communicate directly with Willow, I am enclosing her address and telephone number. Or if you prefer, I can contact her for you and let her know what you wish.

She will be arriving December 19th If you want to meet her, I know it would mean a lot to her.

I understand from Michelle that you and Annette will be married soon. I wish you every happiness and apologize for any grief this letter may cause you.

Sincerely,
Annie

Shane's mind was reeling. How could this be? How could it have happened? His thoughts went back to that weekend...

Sherrie had been so ravishing. His memory adding an ethereal, angelic quality to her beauty. She had been so sullen, but a good sport about their last few days together. She was letting him go. Acknowledging his dreams. But her release of him was not complete. Could not be. Even he felt the tug on his heart, but was ignoring it for both their sakes. He had to be the strong one. He was doing this for the both of them, and if he could see it clearer than her, then the onus was on him to hold steady for their future.

Neither one of them wanted to spoil what time they had left, and so they spent it in revelry, enjoying with wanton abandon the last strains of summer. They swam, and fished, and picnicked and played. They attended an outdoor concert on Saturday night, and drank beer and ate fries.

Later they walked through the park. And made out under the stars. But surely that was as far as it went. They fell asleep by the pagoda. It started to sprinkle... He took her home and went home to bed himself. Oblivious. Oblivious to the act he had just committed. She was so beautiful. In the bloom of youth. So fresh, and alive... and... oh my God...

"Sherrie..." He began to sob, and choke as he knelt down on the floor, still clutching Annies's letter. Shane bowed over and groaned piteously, leaning from side to side. Then all the grief he had never answered to, came calling on his heart, and he yielded to his pent up pain.

He wept. For Sherrie. For her suffering, alone. For his ignorance. His willfulness and stubborn pride.

Because of his grief and shame after Sherrie drowned, Shane had buried himself in his work, using his summers on the island to recoup and pace himself. His art was the only passion he had left. His teaching had became a chore, a necessity, a wheel that kept turning from its own momentum, but without direction or purpose. He had never allowed himself to mourn losing her. He was too racked with guilt when she had died: drunk, out on the sea alone, in a dinghy, at night. He blamed himself then, and even more so now. Only now, he let the floodgates have their way with him. He gave in to the swirling madness and it enveloped him and pulled him into a pit.

Shane wallowed in despair all night, and barely functioned in a stupor all the next day. His thoughts ran along an automatic recycling line that whole day: Sherrie's pregnancy, their daughter, her adoption - Sherrie's death...

He blamed himself for it all. He knew she had resented his working so much that last summer they had together. On one of the last pleasant days of the year he had ignored her calls. He had to work at the gallery. They might not have another opportunity to get out on the water she so loved, but he had good reason for pushing himself. Their destiny depended upon it. He wanted to do right by her. No half measures for him. No life of squalor, or meagerness of any kind. He had to be on the road to achieving his goals, before he could settle down. Of that, he was absolutely sure.

Their last day was a truce of sorts. Neither wanting to spoil it by facing the cruel hard facts. They were too young and immature to deal with reality. So they had acted coy. Acted like nothing as huge as what was tearing them apart was happening. Acted like it was nothing.

The first semester that he was away at university, Sherrie had hardly contacted Shane and he followed suit, throwing himself into his schooling. He broadened and began to grow away from his roots, as well as her. He sensed it, but felt powerless to change it. His second semester, she wrote him once from her aunt's in Saskatchewan. He figured she was broadening her horizons too.

He loved his home and his people. But his summer retreats were always enough for him. He had other dreams too. Dreams that Sherrie hadn't shared. Dreams she had never even seemed to see... and then, she was gone.

Well that was over and done with. What good did it do to rehash the unchangeable? When the offer to teach at his alma mater had presented itself, he took it without regret. Until now.

Suddenly, in the middle of his mournful reflection, a picture of Sherrie flashed through his mind and with it, a powerful paternal thought: her baby adopted out, grown up and living in Saskatchewan...

"Searching for her roots," Annie had said. A girl. A daughter. Willow. His child. She would be twenty three now. He had a daughter. She wanted to know him. He began to think about her. About Willow. About Annie. Annie's understanding heart. And about Sherrie.

By the next night, his love for Sherrie began to comfort him. He began to remember her tenderness, her zeal for life and her love. He knew that she would understand. He knew why she'd protected him to her own hurt. He knew her forgiveness. He also knew that she would want him to know his daughter, now that the truth was out. There wasn't a doubt in his mind that he should be part of the patchwork of sharing that was to infuse Willow with a knowledge of the wonderful, loving mother who bore her.

He would do it. He would meet this child, this grown child, the evidence of a love lost... and found through remembrances and a new awareness.

He decided to phone Annie in the morning. To alleviate any doubt she had over whether she'd done the right thing in writing him. He would phone her, and tell her of the new-found peace and wellbeing he was experiencing. He knew she would understand. He looked forward to the acceptance she'd always held for him, but he'd denied himself from receiving.

For the first time in years, Shane looked forward to going home. And then he called Annette.

CHAPTER SEVEN

TENDERNESS

While Annette was surprised at Shane's news, the woe she had been through in losing her first love, had created a deeper softness and compassion for the wounds and hurts of others. She immediately took in the magnitude of the pain suffered all around, and in her quiet way of faith, let love lead the way. She let Shane know how much she supported whatever he decided to do and that she loved him all the more, for his honesty and humility in admitting his failings.

The wedding plans, while still jubilant, had a sweet melancholy undertone. Annette with her thoughts of David and remembering her first wedding and Shane with his burden of loss and fear for the future. Still, they let their love surround them and those who cared for them multiplied the blessing, until they were both the richer despite their losses.

The ceremony was simple and elegant, held in St. Anne's church on Lennox Island. The chief, the island elders and the priest performed their requisite rituals. Bridgette read a poem and Michelle and Alise sang a precious ballad about the beauty of lasting love. Annette wore a street length ivory organza dress that accentuated her tiny waist and full figure.

Shane wore a black suit with white stitching on the collar, a black shirt and a black and silver string tie with his father's silver/ pearl cuff links. At six foot three, he was an imposing figure, except for the gentle glow in his eyes, the telltale look of a man in love. He was at peace with the world and bittersweet joy was his portion.

A traditional Thanksgiving feast was served at the cultural centre, which looked more like a gathering of the United Nations, given the ethnicity of all the wedding guests. It was a satisfying event for all concerned and a special memory that Shane and Annette would cherish for years to come.

CHAPTER EIGHT

CELEBRATION

Annie made all of the arrangements and Willow arrived a week before Christmas. She stayed with Annie for the first four days, and saturated herself in the Mi'Kmaq culture. She had studied it in university, but she wanted to experience the textures, smells, tastes and sounds of her people firsthand. The village was especially accommodating to this love child from two of their very own.

Annie made the evenings special, by having various guests and events planned for Willow, and before they retired, she and Willow talked long into the night, with lights dimmed and the fireplace glowing between their matching upholstered rocking chairs. Each morning, Willow would make Annie's tea and bannock for her. This simple ritual made the precious days even more special, and Annie wished it never had to end.

On the afternoon of the fifth day, Shane arrived on Lennox Island as planned. He called ahead to insure Willow was ready for him to pick her up. He wanted to take her to dinner in Charlottetown for some alone time to acquaint himself with his child and to let her get to know who he was. She was beautiful, and intelligent; and he marvelled how perfectly she reflected the best of both he and Sherrie. He found himself wistfully tearing up a couple times and was thankful for the candlelight dimness in the dining room that concealed his overwrought emotions.

Willow relayed that she was studying social sciences in Vancouver, while Shane explained that he worked for the federal government in First Nations relations. Together they discovered commonalities and differences between them, but it was only near the closing time of the restaurant that Shane spoke up quietly, "I am so sorry about Sherrie. I loved your mother. She was a wonderful person."

"I know, Dad." Willow said. I can tell by the way you and Grandmother talk about her."

Shane drove Willow home to Shiloh and saw her comfortably ensconced in the guest room, before settling in beside his wife in their suite.

"Is she here," Annette whispered.

He reached his arm all the way around his wife and held her snug. "She's here," he whispered back.

"And she's wonderful."

He kissed the back of Annette's neck and sighed with a smile and silent tears of gratitude on his face.

CHAPTER NINE

JOY OVERFLOW

The next morning, the entire household was at the kitchen table when Willow wandered in. Annette rose to greet her with a hug and poured her a coffee while offering her a seat by Shane. Both girls peppered her with questions about university, boys and Vancouver, while Shane held her hand and beamed. Eventually, everyone settled into a normalized conversation and Willow relaxed, looking at ease.

"I can't believe how picturesque PEI is," she smiled. "Like a greeting card!"

"Well, some parts aren't so lovely," Bridgette exclaimed, referencing the fish docks and the slaughter yards in a rant, while crinkling her nose. "Mind you, under all this snow, even they probably look presentable. Do you ride horses, Willow?" she pressed, while she still had the floor.

"I can. What did you have in mind?"

"Mom, can we?" Bridgette looked pleadingly at her mother, who looked at Shane.

"Maybe for an hour or so after breakfast," he said. "But then, we've got a big day planned," he announced with a theatrical pose.

The day was mapped out with Christmas shopping on the agenda, then a stint at the Salvation Army soup kitchen where later in the day, Willow jumped in with both feet and was soon charming the toothless old grandpas and giving seconds to the thinner addicts. She was obviously a substantial young woman with brains to match her beauty and a heart of gold. Shane couldn't have been prouder. She fit right in.

The next day, everyone snuck around secretively, as gifts were wrapped and goodies were baked. Supper was served in the large formal dining room with all the staff and boarders in attendance. Molly, her assistant, and Annette outdid themselves serving culinary Christmas fare from coast to coast and everyone ate with relish. Annette's eyes glowed with a special sparkle and she couldn't wait to tell Shane of her news the next morning.

After dinner, everyone packed into two vans to attend the Christmas Eve service at Shane and Annette's contemporary Christian church. Traditional hymns were interspersed with modern ditties to celebrate the season, complete with maritime charm. Many folks came over to meet Willow and make her feel welcome. She truly enjoyed the evening and it became part of the tapestry of precious memories she was making during her trip.

Two feet of snow was already on the ground, and a fresh dusting started as they were driving home from the service. It seemed only natural for Alise to break out in a Christmas carol; and after that, good natured joshing followed, over who had a good singing voice and who should stick to shower concertos. Shane told a native legend about a shaman who had found a white baby abandoned outside his tepee in the winter-time and how he had nurtured it and it grew to be a wiseman who delivered their people during a perilous drought many years later.

Peace on earth and goodwill were overflowing at Shiloh that night. And the next day would only get better.

CHAPTER TEN

PROMISE

The next morning, Annette woke first and kissed her husband nibbling on his ear. "Wake up sleepyhead. I've got a surprise for you."

"Wha-What?" Shane covered his eyes and squinted over his arm. "What did you say?"

"Do you want it or not?" Annette gushed, holding out a little package wrapped in silver and white.

Shane grabbed her wrist, pulling her close as he stole a kiss and the package from her hands. He opened it quickly, like a small child would and looked up at her stunned.

In the package lay a tiny pair of moccasins she had purchased online.

"Come next June, we should have a bit more excitement around here than usual," she smiled, kissing his forehead.

"Really? Are you? Are we…?"

She nodded, kissing his mouth this time.

He knelt up in bed and kissed her tummy and then her lips again. Then he shouted. "Wahoo!"

Bridgette and Alise came running into their room, but stopped at the entry, with Willow right behind. James and Molly couldn't see over the crowd in the doorway, but deduced the news from the shrieks and hugs that followed.

Christmas Day was a leisurely day of gift opening, eating, chatting, walking outside and hugging.

Late that night, as they lay in bed, Annette thought of David and Shane thought of Sherrie… and two little babies fluttered in the warmth of their own little world. Love is enough

EPILOGUE

The following Spring, Annie, Shane and Willow commissioned a sculpture in memory of Sherrie. It was a mythical sea nymph in a native motif, mounted on a granite pillar at the edge of her favourite swimming spot. It held a plaque featuring a Mi'kmaq blessing for all who swam there. They also started a scholarship for aboriginal females in her name, and Willow came back every summer to volunteer at the cultural centre and to work in the gallery with her father. She stayed with Annie during those visits, of course.

The twins, Colton and Ami, arrived the first of June, and brought a new liveliness to Shiloh. Annette's time was taken up with their care. Thankfully Alise loved being a little mother and assisted immensely. Bridgette took over many of her mother's responsibilities and an accounting student from the university was hired part time to keep the books. Though he looked more like an athlete than an academic, and Bridgette seemed to find herself in the office more than was really necessary.

The property across the road from Shiloh was purchased and an expansion plan was underway with architects. A campground, go cart track and general store were part of the first phase and a banquet hall with additional accommodation upstairs was planned for the back of the parcel behind the lake in its midst.

Shiloh was featured in a travel magazine for innovation and five star value, and it had won the previous year's Best Business award for the entire Island. Tourists began booking three years in advance. Two former interns were brought on staff to shepherd the expansion project and to keep things running smoothly over the peak season. The future looked especially bright and Annette kept her heart focused heavenward in gratitude for it all. David was never far from her thoughts.

BACKGROUND INFORMATION

Research: http://www.lennoxisland.com

Welcome to Lennox Island Mi'Kmaq First Nation, Prince Edward Island, Canada.

Our Mi'kmaq community is strong, proud and vibrant. Steeped in Mi'kmaq culture and traditions that have been passed down to us since time immemorial, our community has embraced our past and present and we look forward to our journey into a bright and thriving future. Approximately 450 residents call this special place "home" while countless thousands of others can trace their roots back to this fair soil. Generations of Aboriginal people have respected and cherished these lands and waters. Archaeological evidence and oral traditions indicate the presence of our ancestors on the shores of Malpeque Bay dating back 10,000 years. Our spiritual attachment and connection endures here and this place in the Malpeque Bay has significance to us, which all Canadians can appreciate.

For thousands of years, our people have been sustained by the sea. While methods have changed and technology has advanced, our connection with the fishery has remained. Lennox Island currently has 32 boats in the commercial and traditional lobster fishery. Our citizens harvest oysters, snow crab, clams and countless other fish resources. The fishery is our largest employer and we remain eternally grateful to the sea for its bounty. It is with respect, dignity and thanks that our people accept these offerings.

In the Spring of 2010, our community began operations at Minigoo Fisheries , the only Aboriginal owned and operated fish processing facility in Atlantic Canada. This company is owned by the members of Lennox Island First Nation and all citizens will share in its success. We are excited about the potential of this operation, as well as other opportunities for future success in the fishery and other business ventures.

We encourage visitors to come and share the unique Mi'kmaq experience that Lennox Island has to offer. Come take a walk in the footsteps of those who have gone before us on the Path of Our Forefathers. Stop in and learn more about the PEI Mi'kmaq in our Eco Tourism Centre and the Cultural Centre. Enjoy traditional Mi'kmaq food. Make your own Mi'kmaq basket. Visit with our elders and listen as they share the stories and legends of our proud culture. Our residents are fond of saying that "if the Creator made any place more beautiful than this, he surely kept it for himself".

Our vistas are breathtaking. Our people are genuine and friendly. Our community is always open to friends new and old. I encourage you to experience Lennox Island and all that we have to offer. You will be glad you did.

Oelalin.

Author's Note: The small group of First Nations people of Lennox Island are raising funds to restore the heart of their community: St. Anne's Church.

If you enjoyed this fictional story "Island Child", check out the Lennox Island website (www.lennoxisland.com) and donate generously to their church restoration fund:

To make a donation to the St. Anne's Church Restoration Fund, please contact the Band Office:
Civic Address
2 Eagle Feather Trail
Lennox Island, PE C0B 1P0
Phone: (902) 831-2779 or (902) 831-2493
Mail Address:
P.O. Box 134,
Lennox Island, PE C0B 1P0

"Any people who come here from around the world would be welcomed here." Band Chief Darlene Bernard 2012

BETH

For my sister Shelley. This is my story. I wrote it for you. You have never been far from my thoughts, my prayers, my heart.

CONTENTS

CHAPTER ONE

MOVEMENT

[handwritten annotation: → sat on her haunches]

It was mid-morning in early August, during a time before the new world. Beth crouched in the squalor of a pigpen behind a trough, the muck oozing between her naked toes. She ate the still-warm tart that had been cooling in a farmhouse window. The one she had swiped while the matron and her daughter were washing dishes and cleaning the scullery from their morning baking. Her eyes scanned between the back door off the kitchen, and the outbuildings of the premises, to determine if she had been discovered and pursued.

In the dark shadows of this forsaken corner of the earth, she crouched, hugging her knees and pondering her next move. The loft of the barn looked inviting enough, but it was still early and she would have to wait until evening before creeping about.

So she stayed. Still. Quiet. Invisible.

Farmer Jack, his wife Matilda and their seven children soon sat down to eat the Johnson noon meal, jabbering about the price of wheat, the rest of harvest, the life of the royals and the announced arrival of the regent, Sir Anthony of Scarborough, the next fortnight… depending on the sea's mood.

Squinting to see inside the kitchen, Beth could barely make out the Johnson children sitting in ascending ages, like stair steps around the table. The littlest ones were jolly, round and giggling between mouthfuls; whilst jostling and pinching one another under the table.

Though all younger than Beth, three of the siblings were taller and outweighed her demure, seventeen year old frame. She'd seen them earlier, from the edge of the wood, as the younger ones had played down by the creek under the auspices of an older sister Dawn, as she had heard them call her.

Jake and Ernest were seconded to assist their father with the threshing. Mary, the eldest, assisted their mother with the domestic chores, often while singing little ditties. Pondering this made Beth melancholy more than anything else she observed, as she faintly remembered a song she had once sung, before the *disaster.*

Scene
Four-year-old Beth is singing in a sitting room, while her mother accompanies her on the harpsichord. Father enters and joins them in the sumptuous surroundings. He begins throwing Beth into the air and tickling her. Then, he put her down gently, right before Lizzie enters the room to announce supper:
"Cook's made candied ham, sweet potato pie, green beans and blackberry tarts." The young maid recounted this, casting her eyes heavenward while reciting the menu. Then beaming and nodding satisfied at the successful completion of her errand, she couldn't resist a jaunty skip after she half-curtseyed, turned and twirled her skirt before leaving to assist with the serving... That was, until she caught Father's disapproving look and the subtle shaking of Mother's bowed head. This caused Lizzie to pull herself upright and return to her oft-drilled demeanor. Father winked and squeezed Mother's hand, while reaching out to Beth with his other hand.

Beth was snatched from her reverie, when the blacksmith's apprentice pulled up nearby in a wagon. He spent the afternoon re-shodding horses just outside the pen near the trough, forcing her to stay firmly put and out of sight.

Beth debated if, when the young man left, she should sneak into his buckboard and hitch a ride to the next town where he had come from, or linger under the Johnson's involuntary hospitality a while longer. She watched the wagon warily, as she studied the barnyard activities around her. Insects, rodents, birds and kittens paraded past in a lazy fashion all afternoon, as the sun sank lower in the sky.

Later, Beth almost dozed off while watching an ant carry a large crumb home for his family's dinner. She wished she knew where he was going. It would have been easy for her to assist him, but unfortunately she didn't speak ant, so the poor creature would just have to struggle on alone. She followed his tedious journey with her eyes: her head bobbing and her eyelids getting heavier. When a hearty laugh jolted her to attention.

Farmer Jack was paying the boy now and, while slapping him on the shoulder, was commending him heartily for doing such a good job; as quick and as well as his master. He offered the young man some refreshments, and they both walked toward the house laughing and discussing the weather, just as Mary was coming out the back door of the kitchen with a tray of lemonade and cookies.

Recognizing her chance, Beth sprinted for the back of the wagon and clambered under some old blankets, just as the boy turned to leave the farmer and his daughter. She settled into a comfortable position and enjoyed the driver's singing, whistling and horse-talk until the rocking of the wagon lulled her to sleep.

Ordinarily, Beth would have waited until after dark, when the town was asleep before venturing out of the wagon to survey her new surroundings, but her dream, so real, climaxed with a real-world crack of thunder, causing Beth to jump up with a start, just as the stable boy and blacksmith's apprentice were leading the unhitched horses to their barn.

Scene Dream

Father and Mother had been preparing for a journey: maids were dressing six-year-old Beth; servants were packing chests; and footmen were attending to the heavy lifting of loading them onto a large, fancy coach. Later, Beth was in the rolling carriage, seated next to her mother. Her father was seated across from them.

They were traveling on an unfamiliar stretch of road, when their party was besieged by bandits.

The driver and footman were killed in the skirmish and the runaway horses were heading for a drop-off, over a high, steep rock face. At the last minute, Father grabbed Beth and threw her out the window of the coach. Her mother was screaming and

167

then she heard the large crack of the wagon breaking on the rocks below, as she somersaulted to safety.

With both cracks coinciding, Beth was momentarily confused. The stable hands spotted her when she bolted upright in the wagon, but they couldn't let go of the horses to pursue her. The apprentice hollered, "Hey| and "How'd you get in there?" as Beth jumped out and ran toward a backstreet perpendicular to the livery. She ran until she was sure no one was following her, then scooted under a wide spot in the boardwalk.

It began raining, so after that, few folks ventured outside. This afforded Beth a relatively safe haven. Later, when the sky dried up, Beth surveyed her surroundings from behind a rain barrel that she had used to wash up, and surmised that this town was pretty much like the others she had seen. Same general store. Same saloon. Same land surveyors and same white-washed church. She couldn't read the signs over these establishments, but she was familiar with their kind all the same.

Her feet hurt, and after dark, Beth determined she would soak them for a while in a horse trough or stream if she could find one near to the edge of town. Her growling stomach reminded her that she had other priorities to attend to as well, so she continued her keen observation by peering between the buildings and around various obstacles while planning her next actions.

Staying out of sight, until after dark, Beth then poked around for some food, rags, sleeping accommodations, and some form of amusement – such as the tea set left by two little girls on the back stoop of the undertaker's home. The faint glow through the windows of the parlour above created an ethereal ambiance and the warm night air, fragrant with lilac and roses stirred her emotions.

Beth sipped imaginary tea with an imaginary friend and pretended she was back at home with Cook's daughter, Marsha, cuddling their dollies and pretending they were great ladies, having a grand time.

The following days were uneventful except that after being spotted a few times, the town folks assumed she was an idiot child of some outlying squatters or gypsies, and would alternate between feeding her, giving her castoffs and shooing her away from their kith and kin, but of course, she was used to that.

CHAPTER TWO

ACKNOWLEDGEMENT

One morning, Beth awoke in the hayloft of the livery as the first ray of dawn poked at her eyes. Starlings flitted among the stable's rafters as the town came to life outside.

Maybelle at the saloon, had probably left a sweet roll outside her back door, unless she had forgotten again. So Beth slunk along the backside of the main street buildings, crouching below the windows, to avoid detection by the tenements' occupants who were still ensconced snuggly behind their doors. Between the buildings, she spotted some men hanging a banner across Main Street and took note of the extreme tidiness of all the shop fronts.

Folks were out awfully early, sweeping the boardwalk or polishing their windows. An unusual amount of foot traffic seemed to be out earlier than normal too; and everyone was wearing their Sunday best, even though it was only Thursday.

As the day progressed, Beth noticed some men erecting bleachers and welcome signs for the regent's arrival. Beth couldn't read, but she had over-heard the Bounty twins sounding out the words on the banner, while she was eating under their veranda behind the gooseberry bush.

Beth wasn't used to all the pomp surrounding the arrival of such a distinguished statesman, but once the reverie began, her heart swelled with nostalgic twinges as snippets of her own family's arrival at far posts flashed across her memory.

The kindly regent was tall and distinguished looking young man. He reminded Beth of a younger version of her father, what little she remembered of him. He was not yet thirty, she'd wager, and she took the doting elegant woman accompanying him to be his mother, or a matronly patron perhaps.

She laughed when he tipped his hat to the appreciative crowd and flipped it onto his hand, only to roll it back up his sleeve and return it to his head again. Beth liked him instantly and pulled her knees up to her chest, impulsively hugging herself and grinning atop the general store roof, mostly hidden by the chimney. She could safely observe the goings on up there, without making a nuisance of herself.

Speeches were finished and the regent was resorting up the street with some of the local dignitaries. They were headed, no doubt, to the saloon directly across the road from her perch, when he happened to look up and see Beth, who had been waiting for the crowd to disperse.

"She's a halfwit, lives on the outskirts of town," the sheriff offered.

"Don't pay her no never mind," the proprietor of the bank admonished.

He took the regent's elbow and sought to hurry him along. Others motioned, or hollered for Beth to remove herself. She was trying to accommodate them, when suddenly she lost her footing and they all let out a collective gasp.

She was scrambling backward and trying to regain her position, when she slipped a second time and slid off the roof all elbows and knees, completely ungraceful. The last thing Beth remembered was hitting the ground hard and seeing stars.

CHAPTER THREE

BREAKING

Beth awoke in the doctor's infirmary, hearing the regent discussing her case with the doctor and his wife. She turned her head to see them in the sitting room, that doubled as a waiting room, beyond some open curtains. "Sir Anthony, that won't be necessary," the kindly doctor was saying, pushing away a procured bank note.

Anthony insisted and gave specific instructions for Beth's care while he traveled the coastlands for six weeks: after which time, he'd settle any outstanding charges.

There was no misunderstanding his tone, or his instructions. The doctor's wife smiled knowingly and promised her input as well.

Beth's recovery was slow, painful and awkward. When she was finally able to hobble on crutches for a bit, she never went far from the doctor's quarters. As usual, the townsfolk were mostly mean to her. Whether from fear or spite, Beth never really knew, but most spewed out cruel jargon designed to cut and wound.

Contrasted with the doctor and his wife's kindnesses shown by delicious meals, fresh linens, lavender soaps, lace clothing and hair ribbons, these wounds were even more difficult to bear.

In her dirty, hardened state, Beth had endured worse, but now that her dreams were melding with reality and her assumed societal acceptance was not forthcoming, Beth was broken-hearted. Still, she sought to improve herself by paying strict attention to the doctor's instructions, and his wife's reading and writing lessons, seasoned with etiquette, music and levity. She hoped it was working and by the fourth week, a few suitors began to call, but their true intentions were soon discovered and they were dispatched summarily by the doctor, his wife, Beth, or all three.

Toward the end of the sixth week, Beth surmised her need of the doctor and his wife was becoming unnecessary, but she was hoping to thank her benefactor before she left to resume her dreary path. So, timidly she asked the doctor's wife one day, "When will the regent return?"

"Oh, next week or two, I suppose," the now dear woman offered absently, while darning stockings.

Beth lingered a few more days, sure she'd worn out her welcome, but reluctant to change her circumstances, or to miss the regent's return. She often stood at the window, looking up the road, willing him to appear.

The doctor and his wife never indicated that she should leave; or showed her anything but kindness, but when they received a letter from the doctor's sisters, saying they were coming for a visit, his wife discussed it brightly at supper... and Beth felt the death knell of her hope had sounded, since their house was quite small.

That night, she took her few new belongings in a bundle and slipped unnoticed into the dark. She left only two words on a note addressed to the doctor, his wife and Anthony: Thank you.

Beth trudged in the dead of night and headed up the road to a town she had never been to, but had heard tell of a sea port there. Perhaps she could find work in the saloon, or stow away on a ship, destined for a place far from all her recent bittersweet memories. She wondered if she could pull off disguising herself as a cabin boy, but figured her soft, shy, girl's voice would probably give her away.

The road was easy to navigate. It was wide and mostly smooth, and the moonlight was a comforting companion. Beth kept inhaling deep breaths of the cool evening air in an attempt to sooth her ragged emotions and jagged nerves. For travelling out in the open, even at night, was risky to be sure, but she felt somewhat safer under a star-filled, velvet sky, and the cloudless moon-glow. Walking in the woods, had seemed the more dangerous of her two options, so she stuck to the road.

She was lost in thought of what-might-have-been, when three ruffians rounded the bend up ahead and spotted Beth the same time she saw them. She dropped her bundle and turned to run back the way she'd come, instinctively hoping for help... but none came. The inebriated lot overtook her and did their worst.

She fought, and they took some lumps for their trouble, but in the end, they owned her. They were so vicious and the pain was so great, that soon, there were no tears, there was no sound, no movement. Only wishing for death, hoping if she laid still enough it would mercifully claim her. Finally, she fainted from their punishing cruelty.

And so it was how Anthony found her, discarded on the side of the road. He was riding at full gallop from the docks toward the doctor's village, having not even slept or eaten after his ship pulled into port.

He wrapped her in his waistcoat and placed her sidesaddle on his horse. He then mounted his faithful steed behind her and held her firm, cradling her with one hand while gently directing his beast of burden with the other.

It was past daybreak when they arrived on the outskirts of town. Practically everyone noted their arrival as they proceeded slowly, straight down the middle of the main thoroughfare. Many shook their heads and clucked. Others turned away, surmising all too accurately what exactly had occurred. Anthony noticed three n'er-do-wells outside the saloon. They were spitting and shifting nervously, only stealing sideways glances at him, but keeping their eyes mostly downcast, while they muttered imperceptibly to each other.

Anthony correctly assessed their involvement in Beth's predicament, and made plans to have the local constabulary investigate later.

The doctor's house was at the far end of the village. So it took a long time until they arrived. Anthony kept Beth well covered except for her lacerated and bruised face, which was hideously swollen and grotesquely marred. Dried blood was caked in her hair and throughout her body. He was sure that more than a few bones were re-broken. He knew it was her, and even though she was damaged beyond recognition, everyone in town knew it too. Collective shame settled over all.

Beth drifted in and out of consciousness, moaning piteously. She had difficulty breathing, due to a couple of broken ribs. The searing pain wracked all over her body and emotions ran rampant through her unconscious, injured brain, while silent tears made a constant trek down her cheeks.

CHAPTER FOUR

HOPE

It took the doctor the rest of the day to survey and assess the damage: a broken arm, a concussion, cracked ribs, probable internal bleeding, bruises and contusions that required ninety-eight stitches in all. He determined the internal and mental damage to be the most severe. The draught he made Beth drink was bitter, and made her nauseated, but it brought merciful sleep and sweet relief for which she was deeply grateful.

Two days later, Beth awoke intermittently, only vaguely recalling the doctor and his wife's frequent ministrations to her, but it was Anthony, who never left her side, except once to advise the sheriff of his suspicions.

The guilty parties were arrested after several witnesses from the saloon gave detailed accounts of what they had overheard the miscreants discussing none-too-discreetly at their barroom table, past midnight during the night in question. The sheriff corroborated these accounts, with the doctor's report of Beth's injuries and sent for the circuit judge – hoping that Beth would be able to identify the scoundrels by the time he arrived.

She was however, spared this and the indignity of a trial, when all three confessed, albeit, with each one implicating the other two as being the worst offenders. Trial and sentencing was swift and circumspect. Townfolk had no juicy tidbits to chew on, and the no-nonsense judge insured his orders were implemented before he left town, to guarantee the young woman in question endured no further injury whatsoever.

With Beth's healing, came a slowly introduced plan: Anthony proposed to take her with him on his next year's voyage. His reasoning was sound: she needed protection as well as a change; the travel would increase her learning; she had no where else to go; and, he would worry terribly about her, if he could not see to her welfare personally, now that she had been injured twice since he first set eyes on her.

Beth had no reasonable argument, and acquiesced without much of a fight. Her words were quiet and subdued, but her eyes sparkled with expectancy. Despite herself, something in her *dared to believe* that Anthony was as good and as noble as he seemed.

Before the judge left town, Anthony had him draw up papers appointing him as Beth's guardian. He also hired the milliner's assistant, Bonny, to chaperone and assist Beth as needed.

Upon hearing his idea, Bonny, who had a head full of sand coloured ringlets, was slightly pudgy, and very jolly, confessed she had always wanted to travel and readily agreed. And so the arrangements were amicably made.

It was Bonny who selected the travel wardrobes, that Anthony insisted on purchasing, for "Miss Beth" and herself. Now, for the first time, businesses in town were favourable to Beth, for Anthony's sake. As she ventured out with Bonny and Anthony in attendance, folks smiled and greeted her warmly; even if privately they wondered at how taken with Beth, Anthony seemed to have become. Most simply figured he was an unusually generous social do-gooder, and were only too happy to have him bestowing some of his treasure in their coffers.

The day of their departure arrived, sunny and full of promise. Anthony assured the doctor, Bonny's employer, and the shipyard broker that he would return in approximately one year's time.

Anthony personally escorted Beth and Bonny to their comfortable quarters, his own in fact, but he had commissioned them to be decorated to a feminine palate. He would bunk with the first mate and be glad for the delight of seeing Beth well cared for, as she discovered the beauty that is in the world, under his auspices.

Clear skies lasted more than a month as the ship docked almost daily at large and small ports of call. Sometimes much cargo was hoisted on or off the ship, other times, nothing, save an envelope discreetly nestled under Anthony's waistcoat, was secured. No one would ever imagine that these were the most lucrative or important stops made by the vessel.

Beth and Bonny were permitted to explore each destination for the day – with the first mate and their cabin boy as escorts.

Anthony gave both girls an allowance, though Beth's was more generous by far. It took a while for her to get used to shopping. She would debate a purchase so long, then decide against it and move on to another shop, only to retrace her steps to purchase the original item, if it was still available. A few losses in this regard stiffened her resolve to be more decisive at the outset of a purchase consideration.

Sometimes Anthony accompanied the ladies, and took them to his favourite haunts, out-of-the-way tea shops, art galleries, emporiums featuring all manner of luxury items and fashion; all offering rare goods and impeccable services.

Bonny styled Beth's long tresses in most becoming ways, but they had never been cut, and Bonny finally succeeded in convincing Beth to visit a salon for a full beauty regime at the next big commerce center they set in at.

Anthony had no knowledge of such places, but the wife of a colleague kindly directed the entourage to an establishment on the edge of the town.

Anthony and Bonny dined on cucumber sandwiches and petit fours with honeyed tea, while Beth was pampered from head to toe. The matrons were discreet in addressing Beth's scars, and gave her some ointments that would make them become virtually invisible over time. Beth's face flushed with shame as she recalled how Anthony winced, when he had first noticed the ones on her arms.

Beth had also become very conscious of her hands and kept her gloves on during every excursion, but they had to come off now, and the elderly female attendant who ministered to them was so nurturing and gentle in her mannerisms, that Beth soon relaxed under her aura of sweetness. This angel of mercy coaxed out the beauty of Beth's natural expression through her hands and banished all evidence that years of neglect and abuse had caused. When she was through, Beth felt she was staring at someone else's hands and not her own. Yet over time, this little gift dawned on her so profoundly that she began to use her hands more daintily and with suave movements, so that they became second only to the sparkle in her deep blue eyes, in expressing her ardour and sincerity. After that day, everything she undertook was with more confidence, purpose and lovingkindness. It was as if the manicurist had *imparted her own healing gift* to Beth.

Anthony left the parlour briefly, to see to their dinner reservations and to quickly eat a man's lunch; then Bonny left to post a letter to her mother; and by the time she returned, the masterpiece was ready.

Beth donned a new outfit that she and Bonny had selected together for this specific occasion. Every aspect of her beauty had been enhanced to its optimal best. She felt different, to be sure, and she walked down the sweeping staircase aware of a new confidence. She walked slowly behind the matron of the establishment who announced her entrance with grand flourish. Beth then stepped out from behind the curtain which sequestered the first floor waiting room of the salon and locked eyes with Anthony.

He looked at her with such love, acceptance and sincerity that she was *transformed*.

Time stood still. She saw herself through his eyes. A deep satisfied peace filled her being. She had never known such contentment, never knew such a thing existed. She could have stayed like this forever.

Bonny, momentarily stunned herself, rallied soon enough and jumped to her feet, crushing Beth in an exuberant hug. She gushed on and on at how stunning Beth looked, congratulating herself on a well chosen outfit and recounting every aspect of its complementary features to the admiration of all in their presence.

Bonny made Beth turn slowly around to maximize the effect. When she finished, Anthony took Beth's hand and then scooped her into his arms in a warm hug of total acceptance. He kissed her cheeks, and then held her hands, extending both of their arms fully to take a closer look, fully cognisant the effect his admiration was having on Beth's self esteem.

Finally he took her arm in his and Bonny's in the other and advised the young ladies of their dinner engagement and how privileged he was to be able to show off two of the loveliest beauties to the local society.

178

As they exited the stately building, Beth made a mental note that this day of days would become her birthday – she couldn't recall when her real one was anyway, and no matter what happened to her going forward in life, she would always look back at this as the day she was *born again*. She knew her past was forever banished, and she would have a better future because of who she had now become… regardless of whatever life brought. In her mind's eye, she saw a butterfly emerging from a chrysalis and she hugged Anthony's arm in sheer delight. He kissed her forehead and the cool fresh air of the street only served to magnify the trio's joy.

CHAPTER FIVE

RENEWAL

Dinner that night was a sumptuous affair in a regal hotel dining room. Guests in attendance were the community's elite and visiting luminaries, each distinguished in their own rite. Bonny had to force herself not to stare, as she had never seen such exquisite finery in all her life. Sparkling jewels competed with beautiful women, dashing men and an orchestral magnificence that encased the evening with a magical air.

Bonny whispered oohs and ahhs into Beth's ear all night, hardly noticing that Anthony and Beth were unusually quiet, sparking impulses communicating unspoken between them… though they smiled politely and nodded appropriately.

Course after course of wondrous fare was served: savoury soups, crisp salads, hot breads, delicious venison and roasted vegetables, all followed by delicate pastries, pungent compotes and enlivening spirits of all sorts. Anthony and Beth's attentions were devoted to each other, with only brief dalliances to acknowledge a server, or a guest who had come by their table to shake Anthony's hand.

Whether from the warm glow in the room, the effect of the champagne, or the intoxication of being with Anthony in such an ethereal atmosphere, Beth didn't know, but she felt tingly through and through, and couldn't wait for her next grammar lesson to fully commit the memory to her journal.

There was a full orchestra at the far corner of the expansive, marble floored, room, and Anthony asked Beth if she would care to dance. She declined shyly, not admitting that she didn't know how, but desperately wishing she did. She glanced longingly at those already the dance floor, so elegant, so beautiful, so... *free*.

Anthony invited Bonny to join him, and with his astute leading, she looked wonderful, though she herself had stated that she wasn't "much practised."

At Bonny's coaxing, Beth finally agreed to try, and Anthony led her to an alcove off the main dining room. He gently explained the fundamentals of a waltz and so expertly guided Beth, that she felt as if she were floating, secure and serene on a breezy cloud of bliss.

The night ended all too soon, and a waiting carriage outside returned them to the ship. Bonny clambered up the gangplank like a seasoned sailor (hoisting her skirts sufficiently to make good strides), but Beth turned to Anthony and took his right hand between hers, electrifying them both.

"Thank you," she breathed, looking deeply into his eyes. Then she paused, and whispered, "I never knew life could be like this."

Anthony cupped her chin in his hand and smiled. "This, my dear," he said pausing and kissing both her hands, "is only the beginning."

The remainder of the year was spent visiting exotic and unusual places. Beth blossomed under Bonny and the first mate's tutelage, for he had been a schoolmaster before succumbing to the call of the sea. His spirit of adventure ignited her own and she was fascinated by his insight, vision, and knowledge of the world... geography, news, trade and astronomy. Little by little, Beth extracted facts about Anthony, from him. Like puzzle pieces, fitting to form a clearer and clearer image. Beth knew of his family: three siblings, of whom he was the eldest; a hunting dog named Kobu, and his leisure activities of playing the harpsichord and archery. She knew he disliked tomatoes and currants, but had a fondness for chocolate.

And so it was, that one day, she approached the galley, to ask permission and instruction from the Cook, on how to make a chocolate cake. Since Cook said the more you beat it, the lighter and fluffier the outcome, Beth whipped the batter until both her arms ached. She was so excited about her plans for decorating it, that both she and Cook became engrossed in fabricated mechanisms for achieving her vision (based on a display she had once seen in a bake shop window), and they both forgot to watch the oven. Only smoke and a scorched smell alerted them, and despite a slight dryness, Cook sliced off the offending parts and they were able to salvage the remaining cake into a spectacular confection for Anthony's dessert.

Beth instructed Cook to bring it after she, Bonny, the first mate and Anthony had finished supper. Her eyes were gleaming as she timidly confessed she had made it especially for him.

Anthony rose from the table and circled around to Beth. He kissed her on her cheek, and she blushed as her eyelashes fluttered uncontrollably. Bonny and the first mate gave each other a wink and pretended as if nothing had happened.

Anthony ate three pieces of cake before announcing it was the best he'd ever tasted and that making it, as Beth had done – from her heart, was the nicest thing anyone had ever done for him. That he understood her intent, meant everything to her.

Beth knew he cared about her, not the cake, because she could barely stomach the stuff. This made her love him all the more. She had never known, seen, or heard of, such a man. She wondered at his sterling character and wisdom. He was *otherworldly* in his demeanor, especially toward her. She was completely entranced.

This must be what heaven is like, she mused. Perfect bliss. A place of acceptance and beauty. A place of love.

Under Anthony's care, Beth had received an education, culture, poise and decorum, but he had one thing yet to do for her. Written inquiries via couriered interview and data collecting had yielded him very near his objective. In two more days, they would be in Beth's ancestral village, and depending on the outcome, two days after that, she would remain there or be returned to the doctor and his wife's care, until he could make her fully and completely his own dear wife.

CHAPTER SIX

DECLARATION

On the brilliant morning of his objective, Beth could sense a change in Anthony. He barely ate or spoke in her presence and when he did, he spoke with his mouth full, then was silent for long stretches, pretending to read the same missive for an extremely long time without turning the pages. She studied him, but could not for the life of her, discover the reason for his demeanor. Then, suddenly, he cleared his throat and announced stiltingly that he had a surprise for her; that he had discovered the location of her familial home, and that very day, they were to make enquires after her relatives – if there were any surviving members of her family.

Beth was in shock, but quickly recovered and jumped up to give Anthony a hug and a kiss on his cheek. This only undid him more.

She grabbed both of his hands, "Oh," she exclaimed, "how ever did you manage it? I've never been able to ascertain any useful information myself!" She expressed this very enthusiastically, revealing more freedom than during any previous interaction between them and he loved seeing her so free and full of *joy*.

"Well, my dear," Anthony exulted, I have connections, you know." He said this with a mock air of superiority, his index finger pointing aristocratically into the air, and they both laughed at his upturned nose, pursed lips, and closed-eyes pose. They were still holding hands with warmth racing between them and it was Anthony who rallied sufficiently to break the reverie. And with his most patronizing tone, he decreed, "We must be off. We have schedules to keep!"

The magistrate in town was a kindly old man. He scratched his beard, as he listened to Beth's tale, what she could remember of it. "Ah, yes," he slowly recalled, speaking warmly to Beth and Anthony. No one else had come on this precious mission with them. "I remember, the Princess Elizabeth was on a summer's trip with her parents, to visit her namesake aunt... out on the mainland. She was four, or maybe five at the time."

"I was six," Beth interjected.

"The realm never knew what became of them, though numerous emissaries were sent by their kin, no word ever returned. It was like they disappeared some... eleven or maybe twelve years ago." "Their son is lord of the manor now," he said this looking down and shaking his head. "Young prince must be twenty three or more by now, I'd say."

He lifted his head, and raised his eyes heavenward trying to recall. "Though he's not as kindly as his parents, nor you Miss, beggin' your pardon."

He nodded toward Beth, who nodded gently in return, and smiled warmly... then wrinkled her brow, as a twinge of nostalgia washed over her.

"Thaddeus, yes, that's his name," the elder finished, satisfied with his recall.

Beth brightened with a dawning realization, and blurted out, "Yes! I think, I do have a brother! He used to lead me on my pony. I remember!"

She grabbed both of Anthony's hands and he exulted in the successful end to his search. He closed his eyes and sent up a silent prayer of thanks.

"Then there's Princess Milicent," the gentleman mused absently, again shaking his bowed head. "Hardly see her round these parts anymore. Squandering the family fortune abroad most of the time I reckon hear-ed."

He said this in a colloquial way. Hear, then with a punctuated –ed. He proffered a parchment map from a cupboard, directed Anthony to the familial estate's location, and as they left, turned chuckling to himself while doddering back to his desk. "Little Miss is a princess and ne'er e'en knowed it. Tsk, tsk..."

Anthony steered the rented carriage expertly over the badly-damaged roads and in thirty five minutes, they rounded a bend to behold a vast acreage with vineyards and fruit trees flanking both sides of the estate. Beth sat ramrod straight in the wagon seat beside Anthony. Her hands were folded tightly together and she held her head erect. Silent tears of recollection and hope mingled down her cheeks, as she sensed, more than knew, what lay ahead of her.

An Italian fountain sat prominently in front of the main house, while outbuildings in various stages of disrepair, though difficult to discern at first, became glaringly obvious as one approached closer. Beth's attention kept returning to the fountain, where she had spent so many lazy afternoons with her childhood playmate: Cook's daughter, Marsha, her nursemaid, and her siblings.

Snatches of elusive scenes played hide-and-seek with her thoughts. Images of her parents, especially her mother, hung on the periphery, just out of sight.

And then... they were there. In front of the main house. Anthony looked tenderly at her.

She stuttered, "This, this is m-my home."

A shadow crossed over Anthony's face at these words, but he gritted his teeth, determined to expend to the last dregs, every effort to make her happy.

Thaddeous and Milicent were both in residence, but their reception of Beth was cool and guarded.

With Anthony's assistance, Beth pieced together the last twelve years of her life, starting with the terrible robbery and the accident she had with their parents. Her siblings stated defensively, emphatically, that every means was exhausted, to discover her and their parents' whereabouts, but to no avail. It was determined years ago that they must have died and Thaddeous and Milicent were awarded joint ownership of all the family assets and had subsisted on what little remained, as neither wanted to abandon the estate entirely or see it sold.

Anthony was growing increasingly uncomfortable in the presence of these two. They may have come from the same parents as his Beloved, but were as different from Beth as night is from day. His protection of her was pressing him to extricate her from this den of wolves, but she obliviously chattered brightly about their travels, about their friends, and about their experiences.

Careful my lamb, he thought, *if they even suspect my intentions, they will pounce, I have no doubt.*

The once-lavish estate was in shambles around them, most of the fine pieces of furniture had been auctioned off, and their sallow complexions testified that most of this was mostly due to financing the high cost of low living.

"Well, as you can see," Milicent stated, waving her arm with an air of aristocracy, if not grace, "things have not exactly been peachy these last few years around here. The servants have all gone, except for Matilda."

Beth's heart quickened at the name, and at the same moment, the napping octogenarian emerged from her quarters to prepare the evening meal.

She stopped at the sight of the guests and leaned forward, squinting to get a better look. "Bethy, that you?" she queried stepping closer to Beth, who closed the distance between them. She enfolded her nanny in a hug, while kissing her wrinkled cheeks, wet with tears... all the while murmuring, "Nanny, nanny... nanny."

Matilda took Beth's hands and kissed each one. "Bless the Lord oh my soul, the lost is found!"

Beth helped Matilda with the supper preparations, while Thaddeus showed Anthony around the estate.

Milicent brooded in her room, not sure at all that this omen bode well... her sherry glass emptying several times.

The stables were overgrown outside and full of debris inside. Ghosts of yesteryear were all that remained of the groomsmen and prize horses that had been the Master's pride and joy. One lone nag, gnawed on the wooden gate that was barring its exit. Anthony asked if the horse he had secured for the trip, might be unbridled and brought in, and both men attended silently to the task.

Once they returned to the sunlight, Thaddeus led the way to the gardens, which were now weed infested, having long given up their struggle, except for a luscious, white rose bush at the edge of the vineyard.

"Father planted this the day that Elizabeth was born. It seems to thrive on neglect," Thaddeous explained absently. "And over there is what remains of the red rose beauty, planted for Milicent." "My keepsake is this tree," he gestured, using the riding crop, he'd picked up when they were in the barn.

"I used to climb it as a boy."

The branches were all gnarled and grown inward from lack of pruning and proper husbandry.

Anthony surmised it was a fruit tree, but only God knew what sort. It hosted brambles and thickets all around it and one would be hard pressed to get close enough to tell."

Supper was a humble stew and musty well-water, but Beth ate with delight, enjoying her family immensely. She carried the conversation for everyone. Anthony had never seen her so animated.

Little was learned of the estate's destitution or the siblings' antics over the years. Anthony decided Elizabeth would soon enough discover the cold, harsh facts.

They spent the night in dusty guest rooms and by morning, Anthony's sleepless night had served to hatch a plan. After a meagre breakfast of gruel and weak tea, he suggested a stroll around the estate with Elizabeth.

Her hapless siblings watched curiously as Anthony expertly guided her out the front door talking incessantly, so as to prevent any obstruction to his idea. He shouted they would be back by lunch time and led Elizabeth to the first stall in the stables, where his rented mare chided him for missing her evening and morning meals.

Anthony led the beast out to the field and tied her to a tree where she could munch the high grass contentedly. The day was warm and flies instantly surrounded the beast in a buzzing cloud to which she seemed oblivious. Anthony swatted a few away, while Elizabeth waited patiently on the perimeter footpath and admired Anthony's physique as he removed his jacket and slung it over his shoulder.

She laughed gaily, as he watched the silver threads in her summer dress glinting in the sun. Her blond tresses shone and Anthony recalled, they smelled of chamomile and lavender whenever he was close to her.

Elizabeth hugged herself and twirled, just as he approached, then she lifted her skirts and began running down a slope on the property, toward a stream at the back that was shaded in the cool dark under trees and foliage.

He gave her a lead, admiring her beauty and grace, before pursuing at a leisurely pace. Elizabeth was already wading barefoot into the cool water when he caught up to her. The stones beneath the water were smooth from years of caresses and Anthony stood at the water's edge admiring her free-spirited delight as she splashed and cupped water to refresh her face and neck.

He pulled off his boots, cuffed his pants and joined her in the sacred, peaceful stream. Movement had kept it pure. Life was here. So like Elizabeth, his Beth – pure of heart, simple, and alive.

They walked up and down the stream's edge, the soft sand between their toes. She almost slipped, so Anthony took Elizabeth's hand after that. It was the most natural feeling in the world.

Elizabeth pointed out features along the stream that she remembered. Events from long ago and bittersweet memories causing tears to glisten in her eyes. Her fourth birthday had taken place in the backyard above the stream. She and a five-year-old boy had decided to go for a walk in the forest beyond the stream. They had gotten lost and the fear in her father's eyes when he found them had frightened her even more than being lost.

She told Anthony her father was a good man, gentle and kind and quiet, like him. This thought encouraged Anthony and he suggested they walk in the grass awhile to clean and dry their feet. He directed her to the garden and the white rose bush, planted in her honour. Neither spoke, but Elizabeth knelt down and smelled each flower in turn, gentling caressing their petals and letting fresh tears of remembrance heal her soul.

Anthony finally broke the silence, "Thaddeus told me..."

Elizabeth stood and Anthony silently embraced her planting a kiss on her forehead. He then tenderly told her of his love for her, his plans for their future, and his concerns for the skeletons in the closet of her family estate. He pulled her to arms length and studied her face.

Beth acknowledged his proposal with a full on, bold mouth kiss, lingering into many others with loving embraces and gentle caresses.

"Does that mean yes?" Anthony chuckled, when he finally got a chance.

"Yes, oh, yes!" Elizabeth exclaimed laughing.

They exchanged endearments and walked around the estate, with arms entwined, losing all track of time as lovers do.

190

Finally, Elizabeth grew sombre. "I can see things have changed here. It would be good if I could build a relationship with my siblings without them fearing I have come to take something from them," she said earnestly.

Anthony nodded, as her thoughts mirrored his own.

The rest of the day was spent apprising Thaddeus and Milicent of their plans and making arrangements for her siblings to join Anthony and Elizabeth in a month's time, when their nuptials would take place.

When they returned to the ship, Anthony sent an emissary with details and generous provision for all of the arrangements, to spare Thaddeus the embarrassment of requesting charity.

CHAPTER SEVEN

NEWNESS

When the ship docked at its final haven of the journey, Elizabeth was met with many surprises. Much had changed in their absence, and some changes were clearly visible even from the low lying port.

Anthony directed her attention to the hilltop estate which he had commissioned to be built while they were gone. The home was exquisite, everything she could wish her dream home to be. It was high walled, made of grey stone, with turrets and arches and tall paned windows. It was surrounded with manicured lawns and a proper English flower garden. A fountain, even more spectacular than her homestead's, was flanked with angels with a heroine spired in a twirling dance up through the midst.

_by_

feature

Elizabeth's eyes teared up as she gazed at her Beloved Intended with pure, intimate gratitude.

Then Elizabeth looked back through Anthony's spyglass and saw there was a quaint chapel nestled below the estate. "For proper Sunday services," he explained. School children were running across the meadow that ran between the two, heading home after classes.

Many changes had occurred in the village as well, but not as many as had occurred in Elizabeth... She had left a wounded waif; but was returning as an elegant, poised young woman.

Confident and beautiful, to be sure, but as beautiful within as without, with the sort of grace that only love can produce. Most of the townsfolk did not recognize her, but it wasn't long before the community grapevine resolved the mystery of the lovely young woman accompanying the regent.

As Elizabeth faced the month ahead, her mind jostled with clamouring thoughts, but one supremely dominated them all, and she relished in it, rolling it over and over in her mind: *He loves me... yes, Anthony really loves me!* She would shiver all over with goose bumps at this recollection. And she smiled, all the way down to her toes. Her ecstasy was irrepressible and contagious.

Anthony's family arrived the week before the wedding and the night before they arrived, at a private dinner, Anthony informed Elizabeth of his true identity. The following evening, he introduced her to his beloved parents. She could scarcely believe who this wonderful man truly was. Who his parents were. Who she was to become upon marrying "Anthony".

The revelation was almost too much to take in. Yet, their sincerity and love allayed any fear before it even formed, and Elizabeth relaxed into the comfort of a divine destiny chosen for her before time began.

All pain was gone. Sad tears were banished. Joy was the order of the day. Day after day. And finally the day of days came.

It was a glorious June morning that Elizabeth awoke to. Her heart was fluttering, but her mind was clear and serene. Every aspect of her vision was filled with grace and lovingkindness.

Her attendants were her loyal friends who had stood by her: Bonny, the doctor's wife Bess, Maybelle, Cook, her daughter Marsha, and her beloved nanny, Mathilda. Beth was adorned in the finest lace from Spain. Her jewels were diamonds of the highest quality from the dark continent. She mused, recognizing the irony of such things, as she knew them so intimately. Her hair was woven in amazing curls with interspersed braids in a stunning fashion. Everything complemented her natural beauty, so that everyone exclaimed breathlessly upon seeing her. Her smile was almost permanent; warm and sincere. And her sapphire blue eyes glistened dewy and soft, were almost exclusively focused on Anthony.

Her future father-in-law asked for the privilege of walking her down the aisle, as he was already considering her his daughter as well.

Elizabeth agreed, as she could think of no one else who so closely resembled the kindness and character of her own loving father, except Anthony himself. It had been decided that the identity of Anthony's parentage would not be disclosed, so as to not take away from the bride's day. And so it was that a private ceremony was arranged before the reception, which included only those close members of the bride and groom's entourages. It was there that the Elizabeth became the wife of the Prince. It was there that Thaddeus and Milicent and all the rest of Elizabeth's party learned of her good fortune and the bestowing of their own rewards in this regard. Such was the good humour and generosity of her beloved's Father, the King of all the realm.

As for what followed, a grander celebration could not have been contemplated: no expense was spared at the grand hall of the marital castle. Food and beverages from the four corners of the earth were prevalent in abundance. Lighting and sparkle from the finery of all the guests was dazzling beyond belief. Even the servants, most of whom were citizens from the village that wanted to make amends to the new mistress of the manor, were sumptuously attired and generously compensated for their service.

A lavish orchestra played rich music with the exuberance and effervescence of the occasion. At the prescribed moment, well into the evening, Anthony stood, to greet his guests and reveal his heritage.

A hush fell over the ballroom, as a grand trumpet of proclamation preceded his introduction. He held fast to his new bride's hand, giving it a squeeze before he began.

"Ladies and gentlemen, distinguished guests, honoured friends; My bride and I wish to welcome you to the celebration of our love. We ask only that you enjoy the evening to your hearts' content and make complete our joy.

Anthony continued… "At this time, I wish to introduce my parents, King Alfonse and Queen Irridess."

At this announcement, a collective gasp was released from the crowd, then a look of awe, then applause, as heads nodded in acknowledgment to one another, as to the true name of the "regent called Anthony."

The King rose, and his entourage produced his crown and robe, momentarily engulfing him. A similar group of female attendants, also attired the queen, who smiled in deference to their loving ministrations.

The Prince and Princess were also crowned. He, with a jewel encrusted, complexly worked silver wreath. She, in a complementary diamond and pearl tiara that heightened the look of her ensemble to magnificent glory.

A glow from the head table completed the picture, and everyone paused for a solemn moment to take in the magnitude of what had just been revealed.

Then the King spoke. His voice was both kind and strong, filled with authority and compassion for these, a small representation of his subjects.

"It is as if all ages have awaited this celebration of two hearts joined as one, in holy love," he began. "I know Queen Irridess and I have long awaited this joyful day. As have all my loyal subjects throughout the realm.

"I wish to commend my son, on the choice of a most excellent bride. Everything a princess should be: beautiful in heart, and mind and body. Royalty in her own right, blossoming under the acknowledgment of another like heart. Elizabeth will faithfully meet my son, Jeshurun, at all times, with strength of character and loyalty. She will love him, true and sweet, as I know he will her as well.

In honour of their marriage, I decree this a holy day, throughout all my kingdom, for time immemorial: Bride's Day, in honour of my precious new daughter, Elizabeth!"

He raised his glass, and all present heartily followed. Elizabeth stood and kissed his cheek, tears in both their eyes.

Then Jeshurun joined them and shouted, "to Elizabeth". He drained his glass and swept her up in a hug. The queen rose to join them and the crowd rose and applauded for joy, for the implications it would have for their village, for their future, for their children... and their children's children. For the quintessential comprehension that life would never, ever be the same.

196

EPILOGUE

Jeshurun had traveled incognito, doing the king's business in all faithfulness, as it was his own as well. Princess Elizabeth was now the focus of the kingdom; her fashion, her taste in décor, her beauty preparations, her choice of charitable pursuits.

Shelley: I chose the title "Beth" for this story, because you hate the name (your middle name) ~~and because you hate me~~, I love the name, and have always loved you. As you reflect upon it, I pray you see yourself as I do, as He does, as He has caused me to see you. For this is your story as well. It is all of our stories. It is the story of our souls.

There is a clear distinction between our lives before we know the Lover of our souls, and after.

Everything changes. Everything is different. We embark on a journey. A journey into Him. A journey of self discovery. We learn who we are in Him. How He sees us. What His love looks like. And we become what we behold. We become just like Him; with His same nature. The fullness of the words spoken: "Let us make man in our image and after our likeness."

I John 3:1 says **"Behold, what manner of love the Father hath bestowed upon us, that we should be called the children of God: therefore the world knows us not, because it knew Him not.**

2: Beloved, *Shelley*, now are we the children of God, and it does not yet appear what we shall be: but we know that, when He shall appear (or *as He is appearing*), we shall be like Him: for we shall see Him as He is."

We shall be like Him as we see Him as He is (not as He was, 2,000 years ago). How is He now? How is He appearing, to and in, His church, His beloved, His bride, His wife?

This is what I sought to capture in this story: "Beth". May all who read it become ravished by Him. And may they find their true identity, as they see themselves in and through His eyes.

I am my beloved's and my beloved is mine. Song of Solomon 6:3

To order more copies of this book or to contact the author and/or publisher:

In the **USA:**

HeartBeat Productions Inc.
603 Cherry Street
Sumas, WA 98295
email: heartbeatproductions@gmail.com
866.533.4896

In **Canada:**

HeartBeat Productions Inc.
Box 633
Abbotsford, BC Canada V2T 6Z8
email: heartbeatproductions@gmail.com
604.852.3761

HeartBeat PRODUCTIONS INC.

Made in the USA
San Bernardino, CA
11 May 2016